THE PLAINS

First published by Charco Press 2024

Charco Press Ltd., Office 59, 44-46 Morningside Road, Edinburgh
EH10 4BF

A CIP catalogue record for this book is available
from the British Library.

ISBN: 9781913867928
e-book: 9781913867935

www.charcopress.com

Edited by Fionn Petch
Cover designed by Pablo Font
Typeset by Laura Jones-Rivera
Proofread by Fiona Mackintosh

Federico Falco

THE PLAINS

Translated by
Jennifer Croft

CHARCO  PRESS

For Santi and Sole
For Cande and Julita
For Gonza
For Manolo

It was as if
[…]
the landscape had a syntax
similar to that of our language
and as I moved along
a long sentence was being spoken
on the right and another on the left
and I thought
Maybe the landscape
can understand what I say too.

Ron Padgett

JANUARY

In the city, it's easy to lose track of the time of day, of the passage of time.

In the country, it is impossible.

The noises of dusk, the birds as they settle onto their branches, the parrots' squawks, the chimangos' shrieks, the pigeons' flapping wings. Then, out of nowhere, calm. Silence. The sound of a urinating cow, a stream that batters the ground. Another cow moos in the distance. The call of a bull, more distant still. A few dogs barking. The sky on a night with no moon, no stars. It's time to head inside. The white light of the buzzing bulb. I make myself dinner. I take a shower. The water erases the day's sweat, scent of cheap soap, of cleanness. No matter what I do, specks of black earth stay lodged under my finger-nails. I sit reading next to the lamp, to the drone of the insects on the other side of the mosquito net.

Toads on the veranda, a stray bird stirring on its branch, a lapwing squawks.

Outside is dark and formless. The light is soft and warm in the kitchen. In this stillness, a sense of protection, of refuge. The hum of the refrigerator motor.

It cools down. The silence before dawn is at once both dense and crystalline. Nothing stirs, there is no wind. It is a total silence. No cars, no tussling dogs. The only audible thing, sometimes, is a cow's hooves striking the ground as it shifts its weight from one leg to the other.

It's like a block of silence. If anything stirs, it does so stealthily, with so much caution it's impossible to detect, creeping, slithering, delving, careful, controlling every movement.

The sun comes up. The first are the birds, just as soon as the dark starts to dissipate on the horizon. The usual calls, a cacophony that intensifies as the light gets stronger, oranger. Then when the sun is high enough, when its rays filter even and translucent through the branches of the trees, the bees arrive. They buzz around, heavy, in the flowers and the grass. The flies, the blowflies. As the heat rises, the cows lash their haunches to drive away the insects, or they shake their hides.

The battle against insects, against the wild, against all that comes from elsewhere, from outside: things you don't have to worry about, in general, in the city. After a while there's nothing you can do except surrender: live with the flies, with the horseflies, the stink bugs, the frogs sitting right by the door that time and time again, whenever they get the chance, slip inside the kitchen.

On Friday afternoons, my grandparents would come and collect me at the entrance to my school. I'd take a bag. Three pairs of underwear, three pairs of socks, my old sneakers, a nightshirt, two or three books, a spare pair of sweatpants, clothing for being outdoors, an outfit to wear into town.

When I was a child, when I was seven, eight, nine, ten years old, the weekend began on Friday afternoons, on the last streets of the town, at the source of Güero Road, an old road, so old it had been eaten away by the wind over the years so that now it was more like a passageway deep between two earthen walls, like the bed of an ancient trench, sunken into the earth by the force of so many comings and goings, backs and forths, journeys: the wear and tear of bodies.

It was an F100 with a gear stick on the steering wheel, and I rode up front, in the middle. It sank into the dense guadal as it advanced along that roofless tunnel, flanked by those two dirt walls. From above, from the surface, long, dried-out weeds would cascade over the walls.

We drove on at that depth, a shopping bag always situated between my grandma's legs: bread, meat, sugar, pasta. The air vents only open a crack, the windows rolled all the way up to keep the dust out.

Below us, that earth that was very loose and very fine, shifting, almost like a faded grey or brown talcum powder, lighter-looking than sand, almost the colour of chalk or dry bone. And the corn husks that swirled in the ditches, in times of high winds, after the threshing.

Farther along, the ground grew harder, coarser, and the road rose until it ran parallel to a series of wire fences. Then came, sudden and spectacular, the plain: flat, even, clods of earth in a fallow field, cornstalks cut a foot from the soil, a herd of cows with lowered heads snuffling for stray grains between straw and earth.

By then the light would have softened and then turned a fiery orange. The radio would be on, low. At that hour, almost always, a tango programme on LV16, Río Cuarto Radio. On the Rovettos', rising above the line of the horizon, three gigantic Phoenix palms, in the ploughed soil where once there stood a brick house that little by little kept disappearing with every trip, as though the wind were slowly eroding it, in silence.

By the time we got to Hanged Man Road, the uppermost sky would be fading into a cold, hard blue, and my grandfather would turn on the truck's headlights. The last rays of the sun would redden the chañar by the side of the road where an Italian man, driven mad by the war, had hung himself many years earlier, having got lost one night, believing that the newly inaugurated lights of the town – far away, barely a whitish glow reflecting off the clouds – were the flashes of cannons on some brand new battlefield.

Which war would that have been? Which war had the man conflated with the lights of the town? The one that began in 1914? The one in Libya? The one in Ethiopia?

No one remembers what that Italian man's name was, nor what war he had conflated with the glint of a white route, of lights that only ever wanted to be progress.

Or could it have been New Year's Eve in the small town, and end-of-year fireworks dyeing the darkness of the sky?

Various versions of the anecdote remain in circulation.

The beauty of the three Phoenix palms standing alone in the middle of a field, struck by the orange sun at sunset, as though on a poster of ancient Egypt. Fireworks, each one of their crowns. An ecstatic explosion. On each leaf, green tips of a spark expanding, lemon-yellow core when the palm is newly blooming. Gentle orange once the dates hang ripe in their clusters.

The memory of the truck's lights as they revealed the road. The light proceeds metre by metre, devouring the darkness, discovering new tracks in the black.

The texture of an old souvenir photo. Washed-out colours, amber, tungsten, Bakelite, earthenware blue, the flicker, the underwater silence of the image as if it were in Super 8, the murmur of the running projector.

A hare perfectly still in the middle of the road. The base of its eyes reflecting the headlights, glowing red. Then the hare jumps, races in zigzags, clambers up to where the fence is, slips into the field.

I prune the oregano, prune the thyme, compose the sprigs into bouquets, tie them with twine, hang them upside down from a couple of nails in the wall. It is insanely hot, from morning to night, all day long.

Near the aloe vera, under the araucaria, I find the nest of a little black and yellow snake. It's a small hollow, nothing more. It sleeps in there, coiled. Sometimes it sticks its head out into the sun. Whenever I get close, it darts away.

I spade and rake the soil. I prepare a piece of land and transplant some peppers. The heat doesn't let me continue. The sun beats down so hard you can't be anywhere. I lie down on my back on the cold tiles in an effort to take a siesta. Then I go to Lobos and buy a twenty-five-metre hose, a fly curtain, Raid, Manchester Fluid, more seeds. At dusk, I read under the oak, on a thin sheet of canvas.

A man passes by on the road, on a bicycle, in shorts, pedalling slowly, against the stormy sky. Then thunder, but in the distance, almost inaudible. And clouds that only seem to move if you stand still and stare at them for ages. They look like masses of dense, heavy paint, swirls of oil that collide and intermingle. It doesn't rain, and it doesn't cool off. It hasn't rained in a month. The countryside is all yellow, all dry.

Sun at its highest point. That midday silence, when everything – wind, birds, insects – quiets to collect itself, waiting for the heat to subside. Powerlessness because it will not rain. All I can hear is my own footsteps on the sunburned lawn, on the gravel of the path and the loose earth.

Inside, the creaking of the sheet metal and wood of the roof. The countryside charged with electricity in the withered heat of the afternoon.

January heat that scorches everything. The ants eat up the chard. The birds eat up the rest. It doesn't rain, and whatever has sprouted curls in on itself and dries up. Only the sweet corn holds out slightly. I water as much as I can, but I'm overcome by malaise and by fire. Every morning, something akin to despair. Over and over I tell myself that there's a season for everything. A season for sowing. A season for reaping. A rainy season. A dry season. A season for learning to wait, to allow for the passage of time.

Sometimes, when I would get bored or the journey would start to feel endless, my grandmother would tell me stories as we went. The story of an uncle on the Giraudo side, long dead, who would use the corner of the tablecloth as a napkin and, to avoid getting anything on his clothes, even tuck it into the collar of his shirt.

Once he was having lunch at the Viña de Italia Hotel, where he always stayed when he travelled to the city of Córdoba, and he saw another uncle on the Giraudo side who was passing by the window. He leaped up to catch him, pleased by the coincidence, and as he stood, he dragged the tablecloth with him, strewing the cups, his soup, the plates, the silverware all over the floor.

The story of another uncle on the Giraudo side as he was learning how to drive one of the very first cars to reach that area, how one day it got dark when he was on the road. The brother who was with him was barely more experienced than he was, but he offered him tips and instructions as they occurred to him. Suddenly they saw two lights approaching, and the brother told him to pull over because another car was coming toward them. Uncle Giraudo yielded, pulling all the way over onto the shoulder, but it turned out that what was coming wasn't another car, but rather two motorcycles, one next to the other, each with its own bulb to light the way.

The pair continued driving, and a little later, they saw a single light approach.

It's a car with one headlight burned out, said the brother who was acting as co-pilot, and Uncle Giraudo got off the road, waited on the shoulder, and when the light had passed them, they saw that it was not a car missing a headlight, but rather a single motorcycle, with its single headlight on.

Uncle Giraudo said nothing, got into first gear, and returned to the road. They couldn't have been driving for more than ten minutes before they saw two lights ahead of them again.

Two more motorcycles! I'll slip in between, said Uncle Giraudo, determined not to budge so much as a centimetre this time, and that was how they got into a head-on collision with another automobile exactly like their own.

Many years later I saw the same joke in a Buster Keaton movie. Could it have been a coincidence, or did some roving projector make its way to Punta del Agua or Perdices to show black and white movies on a sheet hung in the churchyard? Could my grandmother have seen that film when she was a child, and taken the anecdote from there?

Or perhaps a Giraudo uncle, one of the only ones who had the money to travel sometimes to Córdoba, or to Rosario, might have seen it there in a cinema and decided to make the anecdote his own, telling it to his nieces upon his return?

Lights in the night, automobiles, bikes. Silent movies like dreams and a laughter that explodes on impact, at the crash, the undoing, the thing that splits in two.

And then we would come to the Santa María ranch, where we'd turn left, onto the main road, the Perdices road, which was also an old road, and a deep one, slumped to the side where a broad canal brought water through with every storm from El Espinillal, from El Molle, from Puente La Selva. The Bocha Pignatelli farm, the Gastaudo farm. And all at once, as if out of nowhere, a line of light posts, a narrow road that opened up to the right. Down the first drive lived Juan Pancho and Juan Jorge, cousins of my mother's, my grandfather's nephews. We drove down the second drive.

Arriving by night, the truck's lights sweeping over the sheds, the wisteria. The truck's lights against the garage wall, getting smaller and smaller, more and more concentrated, as we approached. The silence and the black of the countryside once the engine was off. The fluorescent

8

bulb in the kitchen, Uncle Tonito – a bachelor uncle, my grandfather's brother – who'd already eaten dinner and gone to bed, but who had left the light on for us.

Sleeping in the twin-sized bed that had belonged to my mother before she got married, before she moved to the small town. The bed against the wall, under a window. The freezing sheets that felt slightly damp. Shivering until my body was able to warm all the places it touched. Keeping still, avoiding the areas that remained ice-cold. Just barely feeling them with the tips of my bare toes. Immediate retreat.

Sleeping in socks. Sleeping in sweatpants and a t-shirt. Going to pee in the middle of the night, feeling the cold of the tiles that pierced the fabric of my socks.

Things in the dark no longer exist. At night, everything everywhere seems to disappear. All that remains is the house, its interior, its white walls. A house afloat in black.

If I turn on some of the lights outside – the one by the front door, or the one on the veranda, or the one by the kitchen door – what they reach will become part of my world. I'll look out the window and, in the amber light of those bulbs, make out three to four metres of scorched grass, but then the light peters out, and darkness shifts into matter, takes on heft.

On the other hand, if I don't turn on any lights, when I look out the window, my eyes, adjusted to the darkness, instantly perceive shapes and contours. The eucalyptus and oak trees are black bulks backed by a sky of deep but luminous blue, with just a smattering of stars. If there aren't any lights on to distract me, the darkness turns diaphanous.

I sit on the veranda with the light off to keep away the bugs, and I recap the day's activities. I waited too long to thin the radishes, and now they're grown, their leaves tough. Their roots, instead of digging down into the earth, instead of thickening into bulbs, are just red creeping strings. I planted them densely, haphazardly. Next time I'll plant them in rows and thin them as soon as possible, when they're still seedlings. Now I feel guilty, for bringing them into the world in vain, for not knowing what I was doing.

Almost nothing came up in the bed by the orange tree. Not so much as one zinnia from the seeds my friend Vero gave me, although I'd had such high hopes. And no sunflowers. Just a couple of pincushions, but it's too late for them to bloom this year, even if the heat doesn't completely destroy them.

The birds have eaten up all the chard I just transplanted. Some of which also turned out not to be chard, but rather chicory, which I had not planted. I bought a net to put over the largest garden box and some plastic mesh I plan to use to cover the little side beds. I have to protect what I plant from now on. Everything is so dry, and the birds have so little to eat here that they're capable of wreaking real havoc. They've even been nibbling the lone zucchini seedling that grew.

Meanwhile, I carry on marking out, carry on digging beds. Now, after everything.

The dream of a place to plant forever trees. Creating a garden to last, to extend over a period of time. Zapiola as a dress rehearsal for that dream. Renting this house in the countryside, piecing myself back together, committing to this for a couple of years. I can't plant peach trees or bougainvillea, or any perennial shrubs, but I can try out some annuals, seed plants, the kind that last just one season: this season, my season, the season I'm living in now.

I can't have fruit trees or asparagus or raspberry or redcurrant bushes, but I can have a vegetable garden, to sow in the fall, to sow in the spring.

A dress rehearsal for a garden.

A dress rehearsal for a vegetable garden. A place to pass the time, and to start over.

Now I'm tired. The vegetable garden is tiring. As soon as night falls, I'm asleep. I don't have the energy to think. There's no room for anxiety or sadness. Exhaustion dulls; the earth unburdens. For tomorrow the forecast is heat. I'm going to stay indoors, start reading some simple novel, something that's pure entertainment, something that doesn't require me to focus. I need to go to Lobos for ant killer, but that will have to wait. I should also take advantage of the moon to plant the carrots and leeks. But I'll do it next week, or the week after, or when the moon starts waning again: from full to waning moon is when you sow everything that ought to grow under-ground; from new moon to waxing is for all things leafy, whatever will grow above ground; from waxing to full, fruit producers; you don't do anything from waning to new – you simply wait.

It's getting light out. That beautiful time of day, after the dusty dawn, in the soft, clear light of early morning. Everything is fresh, cerulean, and ample. In the beds and garden boxes, patches of darker earth from last night's watering can still be seen. The birds' first ebullience eases into a serene semi-silence, a few songs overhead, and buzzing all around and underneath, sounds that only foreground the silence, making it more present.

Calm. Silence.

It hasn't rained yet, but it is a perfect morning.

FEBRUARY

In a vegetable garden, there are two seasons of intensive planting: spring, for the summer garden, and fall, for the winter garden. February isn't an especially good time to start a vegetable garden, but I need to do something, and I'm not willing to wait until March to start planting broccoli and cabbage that even in the best-case scenario I won't be eating till the end of November. So I spade the soil, build beds, try, test things out. It's too late for tomatoes, for hard-shelled squash, common or crookneck pumpkins. Too late for bell peppers or chilies or eggplants. Zucchini, on the other hand, and green beans, and chicory, and lettuce can all be sown throughout the summer, as long as the heat is not extreme. Once they've sprouted, they'll fruit until the first frost. Swiss chard and beets can also be planted year-round, summer or winter. 'The thing is to keep busy,' Ciro told me. 'Take your mind off things.' So I try, and I sow.

In December, when I came to view the house, before I'd decided whether to rent it or not, in the place where at some point, a long time ago, there had been a vegetable garden, I came across some woody thyme and oregano, the pompom blooms of six or seven leeks and, lost among the tall grass, three little tomato plants stretching up and up in an effort to escape the suffocation of that overgrown lawn. They hadn't been planted on purpose, they were just the offspring of tomatoes that had fallen, unappreciated, to the ground.

Then when I went back, in early January, now determined, having signed the rental agreement, the owners had had the grass mown across the property, and of the three little tomato plants, only one remained. The mower's blades had finished off the other two, whose stems were still visible, shredded ten centimetres above ground, but the third had slumped over, and the mower had passed above it without doing any harm, had only flattened it a bit, but hadn't cut it. I weeded, cleared the land and removed the surrounding soil, added compost and earthworm humus. I put in a stake. The tomato plant grew. It put out more shoots, two or three more. It had so little body and so little strength that I couldn't bring myself to prune the new shoots, and I simply let them grow. And the plant grew. When it reached my waist, it put out its first cluster of flowers. Now its first tomatoes have arrived. Little ones, only a little bigger than cherry tomatoes, perfectly round.

I ask Luiso about them.

Those are Chinese tomatoes, he says. The owners of the house got the seeds from a friend of theirs who went on a trip to China.

So now I think of them as Chinese tomatoes. I like to look at them. Six little green balls hang from the lowest cluster. From the next, just slightly higher, four. And the plant keeps flowering, stretching out and up.

Luiso comes every day at seven in the morning. He arrives by bicycle, and he leans his bike against the gate in the shade of one of the poplars that stand around the edge of the property. The first thing he does is check the tanks, hook up the pump, and fill the drinking troughs. All the sheep and the five cows and three calves that graze on the fields all around me are his. Where I'm living is in fact the former farmhouse of a modest farm. I'm only renting the house and – the yard? the garden? the plot? that surrounds it, while Luiso has rented the rest: the little pasture and the fields and a small shed where he keeps all his things. The shed is right next to my vegetable garden, on the other side of the fence, so every morning, when he gets there, he finds me with my cup of coffee, inspecting my beds, not fully awake yet. We chat. Luiso with his elbows resting on the topmost wire, smoking his first cigarette, me drinking down my coffee in little gulps. We almost always talk about the weather, the heat and when the forecast says there might be a storm. We also discuss my plans for the vegetable garden, which is a subject that interests Luiso. He tries to figure me out, asks questions I know are to help him evaluate me. He can't quite make up his mind: he doesn't know if I'm a city slicker with no clue about anything or if I might actually know what I'm doing.

I used to garden with my grandparents, when I was a kid, I tell him.

Sure, Luiso says and nods, as if to say, 'We'll see.'

There is a road that passes behind Luiso's shed. That's where the farm ends, and immediately, on the other side of the road, you start to see amid the weeds a group of half-abandoned structures: sheds, silos, old hoppers, trailers. If I look over the hedgerow of privet and evergreens I am able to see them. A while ago, a long time ago, Luiso tells me, there was a cheese factory there. Now that whole area's been abandoned, and then over there, on the other side of the farm, they've put in a pig farm.

That's why sometimes when the wind blows from the south the house is hit with a swinish smell that gets into everything. Swine smell. Fermented food smell. Shit smell. It doesn't bother me. In my small town, when I was a kid, whenever there was a south wind, the air would fill with the smell of the Guastavino pig farm. 'The weather's going to change, you can smell the pigs,' people used to say at the bakery. 'It's cooled off, didn't you notice the pig smell?' the women would call to each other as they swept the sidewalks.

So this smell reminds me of that one, makes this house feel more like home, hastens the passage of time.

Zapiola fauna (to date):

A tabby cat that prowls the roads, sleeps in the firewood and comes up to the house to rip open the garbage bag or lick the steak pan when I leave it outside so that the smell doesn't overwhelm the house.

Two hares that tend to sleep between the trunks of the white acacias at the entrance to the property and that always graze a little on the road first thing in the morning.

A weasel I have only seen once so far, climbing the oak tree.

A little yellow and black snake.

A lot of birds: chimangos, parrots, and some extremely confident mockingbirds that dig around in the bed where I just planted my chard, right before my eyes, a short distance from where I'm standing.

A big old iguana that lives in the pump room. And another smaller one that lives under the root of a dried-up chinaberry tree. And I think there might be a third – or a fourth – under the concrete slab behind Luiso's little shed, near the mulberry tree.

A day of rest, a day of lounging around. After all my digging and clearing, my legs hurt, my back hurts. Drowsiness, a slight burning in my eyes, my joints somewhat swollen, my arms numb. An exhaustion I can't shake. Outside, a roiling sun, an incendiary heat. Even the nettles have dried up, nothing green remains. Dust on leaves. The smell of sun-baked grass. The only things that move are the iguanas that plod across the lawn. If I get close, they race off and hide. They're agile, dinosaur-like. Not a single cloud in the sky. It hasn't rained in weeks. There is no other option than to surrender to summer: between noon and six, there's simply nothing a person can do. In the country, unless you have a pool, summer is time spent indoors, in cool darkness, waiting for the sun to go down, for the golden hour to arrive, for the fiery hours to pass. You air out the house for just a little while, early in the morning, and then, the second the heat starts to rise, you close everything up very quickly, so that the darkness will trap and keep the cool.

The pleasure of not doing anything, semidarkness at siesta hour, reclining to read on the floor, back bare against cold tiles. Waiting for the heat to pass so that, when it gets dark, you can open the doors and windows again, pray for even the slightest breeze, for it to get cooler.

Zapiola is the kind of small town that never quite came to be, or not entirely. A row of houses that face the train station. Two café-bars that are also general stores, Zito's and Anselmo's. Most warn against Zito's, because his prices are high, his scale is rigged, and if he

17

gets a good look at you he'll tack on an extra twenty percent. Then there are four empty fields that are criss-crossed by two dirt roads. Six or seven hundred metres of just grassland and weeds, the horizon all the way around, and, on the other side, 'the other downtown': the square, fenced off by five lines of wire so no horses get in; the chapel with its Calla lilies, daisies, Indian shot; the oldest house in town, which collapsed a while ago and is now just a pile of bricks; a little farther down, the butcher shop, which belongs to Oscar and his wife Cristina.

A handful of solitary constructions, scattered among the fields, in direct sun, without shelter. A broad, horizontal town, a bit unrealistic looking, more lots than houses, more emptiness than town. As though someone had begun to pull it up to move it elsewhere but then forgot about it, leaving it there, in the sun, near to nowhere, surrounded by nothing but earth.

What's the difference between a field and an empty lot? In Zapiola, it's difficult to say.

The clear, broad streets, defenceless against the enormity of the landscape, the enormity of the sun beating down. The trees cannot manage to make shade, nor to free themselves from the soil.

'Places with incomplete combustion,' Alicia Genovese calls small towns like these in one of her poems.

Luiso lives in Zapiola, facing the square, catty-cornered from the chapel. Every day he rides his bike to where I am. It's three and a half kilometres, it takes him twenty minutes. I prefer to walk into town. If I take the bigger road, the main road, it takes a bit less than an hour. But I like to take the back road, which is a little overgrown and rarely used. It's higher up and has better views, and, because almost no one ever passes by, there is less chance of winding up engulfed in a cloud of dirt. The only problem is it takes considerably longer. If I go into town by the back road, it takes me an hour and a half. Ten kilometres of visibility the earth offers before curving, brimming with blue sky. A single massive cloud casts a shadow over a field, showing the magnitude of the expanse of what surrounds me.

Back when I didn't know whether I would rent the house or not, I called Ciro one afternoon to ask if we could meet.

What for? There's nothing new to say. Nothing's changed, he said. I feel the same way I did a month ago, a week ago. We'll just end up saying the same things we've already said a thousand times, and we'll make each other feel bad. Again.

I insisted: I need to talk to you. I need your advice on something.

Fine. Just don't come over.

No, I said. It would never have occurred to me to come over. I couldn't walk through that door again now, I couldn't bear it, it would destroy me.

We agreed to meet at a café. Ciro came on time. Somehow, in the two months since we'd last seen each other, I had forgotten how he looked – how he looked now, as the person he now was. That whole time, whenever I had thought of him – which was almost always – I had remembered him as the kid he'd been when we'd first met: just a little skinnier, less muscle on his arms, more hair and a smoother face, his jaw and cheekbones less pronounced.

Suddenly seeing him restored to his real age made

me feel all at once all the time we'd spent together, an enormous block of time – of life – right there, pressing in on us, like gravity acting on our bodies. It made me very sad.

He'd got new trousers. Something different from the jeans he'd always worn. I also didn't recognize his shirt.

Looks nice on you, I said.

Thanks, he said.

Life went on, and he wanted to look nice for other people now.

I ordered some coffee. Ciro said he'd already had several cups and asked if they carried Pepsi or Coca-Cola. What was it you needed to talk to me about? he said.

I told him how I'd seen this house out in the country, how the rent they were asking was comically low, how I was thinking of taking it.

I'd like to have a vegetable garden, I told him.

What about your workshops?

I cancelled them. I'm not up to it.

Ciro looked at me for a second.

That's crazy, he said. That's insane. What are you going to do there by yourself all day?

I'll have a vegetable garden, I'll eat what I harvest. I want to get some chickens, too.

Ciro moved his head from one side to the other.

The only drawback, I said, is that it doesn't have a phone line. And you can't get cell service there, if you don't want to be completely cut off you have to go into the town.

Ciro repeated his head gesture.

What you need to do is rent a nice apartment and get down to writing, finish those short stories you had started, put together a new book, he said.

I can't right now. I wouldn't know how. Something broke. I don't understand anything. I'm not capable of writing anymore.

You shouldn't have cancelled your workshops, Ciro said. You should be teaching more, creating new courses. You like doing it, you enjoy it. You need to do something you like, something that keeps you busy, that prevents you from getting too much in your head, that helps you pass the time.

I stirred my coffee and didn't say anything.

I need to start over, see what comes next, I said.

What are you planning on living on? Ciro asked.

Our place, I said. I put in my money for the renovations, to build our bedroom, the study, the top floor.

I can't pay you back right now.

Whatever you can do, I said. Even if it's only part of it, you can transfer a little each month.

To help me get through those first few weeks, some friends had loaned me an apartment that ordinarily they rented out. It was an apartment with a lot of rooms, on a high floor, on the older side, but with a lot of light and a full view of the city, lots of sky. They had long since moved to a suburb of Buenos Aires. The apartment barely had any furniture. A mattress on the floor, a pan, an electric kettle. Two or three times a week someone from the real estate agency would call to let me know what time they'd be by the next day. I'd let them in and listen to the same young agent reciting square metres, praising the spaciousness of the closets and the benefits of boiler heating. He almost always showed the apartment in the afternoon, or at lunchtime, almost always to women who came alone, who would inspect the shower, open and close doors, ask where the sun came up and where it set, if the apartment got very hot in the summer, whether the windows let in drafts.

I'd have to come back and see it with my husband, they'd say.

Once a woman came alone holding a baby. She gave only passing glances to the apartment's different features. The only question she asked was how much the monthly bills would be. She didn't mention a boyfriend or a husband or a partner. She spent a long time standing in front of the window, petting the baby's tiny head. Then she asked if the rent was final or if she could get some kind of discount.

I like it, but I don't have the money for it, she said.

The young agent assured her it was something they could talk about. He asked her if she had good references, pay stubs.

The woman didn't seem to hear him. She didn't say anything. She turned back to the window. She cradled the baby and whispered to it under her breath as though it had started crying and she had to calm it down, but the baby was perfectly still, and silent. The situation was becoming uncomfortable. The agent and I exchanged glances.

Is this yours? the woman asked me then, indicating with her eyebrows the walls, the windows, the whole room.

I shook my head.

Who used to live here?

Some friends, I said.

It must be nice to live here, the woman said.

It isn't mine, I repeated.

The woman nodded again.

They must have had a nice life, she said.

Dirt on your skin, dirt in your hair, dust in your ears, your nose, your mouth, your teeth. Dark hardened mucus. The cornfield. The leaves of the corn, scratchy, cutting, rough as sandpaper. The itchiness of grass on your back, your arms, your neck when you lie down on the dried-out lawn. Dry mouth, dry eyes, dry skin. Rheum. Heavy flies that incessantly perch on your skin, insisting. The mosquitoes, the horseflies. Nature demands work.

Dawn. And then suddenly, in an instant, in between the long shadows that are formed by the trees and the house, the light shifts from a warm, enfolding gold to very white and very hard. In sunny spots, the dew dries up. Dawn is over before you can pinpoint the moment the day is fully underway. The sky to the west is a clear, light, vibrant blue. Creamy blue, ceramic cup blue, azulejo blue. By eight in the morning, the temperature has started to climb.

Heat, low atmospheric pressure. The ants have eaten the chicory that had just started to sprout. Two of the little Chinese tomatoes have vanished, the ones that were lower down, one of them ripe already, almost completely red – it would have been the first tomato of the season – and the other still green. I suspect it was an iguana that ate them, although I don't have any proof. Foul mood on an oppressive evening. Dense silence, the kind that comes before a storm, but they're saying it's going to be hot until at least Sunday, with no chance of rain. Spirits in knots, a sweaty, sticky mess.

Another day of intense heat and a lot of wind. It hasn't died down for a second. Everything is well past dry. The wind howls through the eucalyptus, the white light of afternoon hurts. The heat these past few days has been too much. The ants eat the chicory and anything else they can find, the birds eat the chard, the lettuce won't grow, the radishes won't grow bulbs.

Drought. It's about the only thing anyone can talk about. It's been more than two months since it rained. 'We'd need a hundred millimetres, and it'd have to come down slow,' said a man at Anselmo's today, while I was buying detergent, some olives, cheese.

With every trip into town, I've been demarcating the pampas slowly. Little by little, landmarks emerge, divvying up the landscape and helping me put it into words: the abandoned house with the tree that grows inside it (which instantly gives that smaller road its name: Abandoned House Road). The chicken farm, the duck pond, the brick ovens, the little hill with the poplars, that field that runs up against the tracks that is so covered in trees it looks like a block of forest cut out and deposited here, in the pampas, like a piece of cake, a rectangle of forest.

The wind licks the main road, piles up the dust along its sides. It's mid-morning, I'm walking back from town with a couple of steaks and a bag of sugar in my backpack. The most difficult question is what to call those spiralling gusts, vapours of earth the wind raises up from the guadal as it smooths and polishes it. Whirlwinds? Small tornados? Teeny-tiny twisters?

Later, when the wind dies down, in the ditches, at the edge of the tracks, there are some striated mini-dunes that are impossible to describe. They're like sand dunes, but in a satellite photo. Or like the sand on certain beaches, when the tide goes out. What could a person call those earthly waves? They only last a little while, and they're nothing named by any word that already exists.

The ground is split by finger-width cracks nearly five centimetres deep. I've been seeing them for days now, zigzagging around the lawn, near the chinaberry tree, by the veranda, at the front of the house. I thought they were abandoned anthill tunnels that for some reason had had their roofs cave in. I mention it to Luiso.

No, he tells me. It's the earth coming apart because it's too dry.

For the whole of the coming week, the forecast is for temperatures that will always hover over thirty degrees, with highs of thirty-seven, thirty-eight, thirty-nine.

Tomorrow I'll get some seedlings into pots so I can set them on the veranda, where I can keep a closer eye on them, chard, leeks, green onions.

I spend all my afternoons watering, and it's never enough. It's not the right time to be doing anything. With the drought and the high temperatures come a thousand infestations, and everything is an uphill battle. Ants, birds, caterpillars, creepy-crawlies everywhere. Something has been nibbling at the corn, which was tall already, but which is now cut in half. Despite its partial shade, the lettuce I planted three weeks ago isn't making any progress. The heads are small, sparse, just vegetating, frail. Between yesterday and today, the ants have brutalized them, too. The sun has wilted half the chard, the ants ate the other half. One of the plants, measuring almost fifteen centimetres, had survived, but today it was completely gone, not even a trace of where it had been. Birds? Ants? I have to wait for the worst to pass, for different times to come.

Record-breaking heat, historic drought. I shut myself indoors to plan my sowing, sketch out my garden, the layout of the beds, my dream is to install a drip irrigation system, and I put together a whole

map of where all the pipes would go, how many centimetres apart to place the sprinklers, how many U–bends
I should buy, how many T–connections, how many feet
of black pipe. How wonderful it is to make plans. The
problems start when reality, with its heatwaves, its ants,
its infestations, hits.

From the house you can see the trails of dust from
the main road, every time a truck speeds past. The dust
clouds rise and rise, grow, float over the fields. The sun
wilts everything that emerges over the surface of the
earth. Nights are barely any cooler.

Those first few weeks in the borrowed apartment,
I hardly slept, if at all. A couple of hours a night, tops.
Intermittent, broken–off dreams. I'd toss and turn on my
mattress late into the night, get up, go to the bathroom,
check my phone, read for a while, look out from the
balcony at the few windows that were still lit at that
hour, in the distance, lie back down, try some breathing
exercises, count backwards, stay still. My mind would
chew over the same things again and again. Everything
that had turned out badly, not knowing what had
happened, not understanding why. Everything I needed
to do: cancel the credit cards and close the joint bank
accounts, transfer the utilities that were in my name to
Ciro. Change my address. Get off his insurance.

Little by little the light of the new day would filter
through the blinds. The elevators would start to hum,
very occasionally. First around five–fifteen. Then, closer
to six, people opening and closing doors, rapid steps
on the staircase. In the apartment next door, there was
an office, and at six–thirty, the cleaning woman would
arrive. I could hear all her movements clearly through

the walls. The sound of dishes clattering, taps turning on, the sound of running water, the vroom of the vacuum.

Every day I'd go to the same café for breakfast. It was a bit of a bougie café, more of a ladies-who-meet-for-tea type of café, but it was the only one that was open at seven, that was nearby, and that did good coffee.

At that hour there was almost no one there, I could always sit at the same table, and the waitress would bring me my coffee without my having to ask. I'd take a hardcover notebook with me, and I'd write. For hours, without stopping, without even getting up to go to the bathroom, I'd write until I discovered that all the tables around me were full, and there was a general din, people coming in and people leaving. Then I'd ask for the bill and go back to the apartment to see the sun moving in angled boxes over the bare parquet of the rooms, of the hallway.

I never went back and read that notebook. I still have it, in a box I haven't opened, along with the rest of my things, on the table I built to be my desk, which I don't use.

In a furious, cramped, rapid hand, I'd repeat, page after page, over and over, the same thing. My regrets, my complaints. Why me, why this. What I considered my fault, and what I considered Ciro's. Things I wanted to tell him when I saw him, precise transcriptions of our occasional conversations over WhatsApp. The long messages I'd send Ciro, though he didn't respond. Or he only responded sometimes, just one line: 'It's late. This is bad for both of us. Let's take care of ourselves. Don't obsess. Go to sleep.'

Are you a writer? the waitress asked me one morning, indicating my notebook.

I don't know, I said.

She burst out laughing.

What do you mean you don't know? Are you or aren't you?

I don't know, I repeated.

So what are you writing then?

I shrugged.

I used to be a writer, I said.

Here the landscape predominates, contaminates all, invades all – all is landscape. Even in the afternoon, at siesta, with the house closed up, in the dark, it is impossible to forget. Even without opening your eyes, even asleep, the circle of the surrounding horizon never ceases to be felt.

That great empty space.

Here there is no place to rest your eyes. You appreciate any eucalyptus, any utility pole because it helps to stabilize your gaze.

The world is so vast it might seem there is nothing to see: just sky, just fields, things that always look the same.

It is only on making the effort at a closeup that particularities begin to appear, little differences. If you drive four stakes into the ground, if you mark off with red twine a perfect square of one meter by one meter, everything that until a moment ago was just grass will now extricate itself, take shape: bunch grass, Bermuda grass, purple crabgrass, purslane.

And there are grasses without names, or I don't know them. But it doesn't matter. It is as though just looking at them is a form of baptism, as though that alone will suffice for me to start to recognize them now.

Out here, everything is dominated by the landscape, and these days, the landscape is the landscape of drought.

'Remember Monica Vitti saying, I can't watch the sea for a long time or what's happening on land doesn't interest me anymore?' Anne Carson asks. I set what I'm reading face down on the Bermuda grass and think.

But I don't remember. I saw that movie decades ago, as part of a film club, right after my arrival in the city of Córdoba, when I had only just escaped my own small town. I was living in a boarding house, near the Hospital de Clínicas. I'd got myself a job at a construction company, where I was supposed to take old documents off the shelves, opening up folders and files to photocopy them, one by one, and then put the originals back where they had always been. In the afternoons, I would go to the university. I had chosen two subjects: Philosophy and Literature. I studied all the time, and if I wasn't studying, I was reading. Any grade below an A embarrassed me, wounded my pride. I only knew a couple of people in the city, I didn't have any friends yet, I barely talked to anyone. The film club was called The Blue Angel. I went every night and as soon as I got back to my room I'd write down the title of the film, a detailed synopsis, and some small structural analysis: first act, second act, third act. Turning points. Main plot, subplot. Resolution. Conflicts.

I did the same with all the novels I read: I wanted to understand how to tell a story, how to organize the scenes, how to give them meaning.

I wanted to write, but I didn't feel like I was ready yet.

I thought that before I began I would need to know more, study, learn a gazillion things, and only then would I be able to say: I'm a writer.

Act One – get your hero character up a tree,
Act Two – throw stones/rocks at him, and
Act Three – get him down.
A structural analysis by the screenwriter of *Casablanca*.

The hero's journey: the quest to attain an impossible-seeming goal, with the help of friends and allies, facing trials along the way, defeating enemies and learning and transforming in order to arrive at a final confrontation, where everything that has been learned helps – and becomes essential – in the hero's triumph.

The romantic comedy: Boy meets girl/boy loses girl/boy gets girl back, and they live happily ever after.

Rags to riches – the search for happiness: from pauper to millionaire/from millionaire back to pauper/from pauper to millionaire for the second time, but now having learned how to live a good life, as in, for example, Cinderella.

The stranger/outsider who arrives in a town and is perceived as a threat, suffers initial rejection, becomes a) a source of terror to the community, seeking revenge – the monster; or b) a source of healing and wisdom – the shaman or the catalyst of change.

The journey to a strange land and the return from that journey. The protagonist is sent to a distant land

– real or fantastic – where he will have adventures and learn new ways of seeing and acting in the world and then return to his place of origin, older and wiser, to share these new ways.

The love triangle. Revenge. The best friend's betrayal. Forbidden loves. Facing the darkness. The monster that lives inside the protagonist. The halfway point of the plot that foreshadows the outcome of the final confrontation. If at the halfway point the protagonist feels that all is lost, it is because he will triumph over the bad guys at the climax. If at the halfway point the protagonist feels like he's on top of the world, it is because he will be brought to his knees in the last chapter or last quarter of the film.

I was afraid to write, I was afraid I wouldn't be as good – as original, as entertaining, as intelligent – as I thought I needed to be, as I wanted.

I was desperate to be someone. Desperate to read a newspaper review that said my name and, next to it, the word 'great'.

Let them read that in Cabrera, let them read that in my little town.

'I can't watch the sea for a long time or what's happening on land doesn't interest me anymore,' said Monica Vitti.

All I want now is to watch the horizon, the plains, to stare into the distance, let the countryside inundate me, let the sky fill me up, not to think, so that what is happening inside me stops existing all the time.

One day we went to buy a table for the living room. It was a used table, we'd bought it online. We loaded it into the car, brought it home, set it in front of the couch. We set some books on it, some little objects, souvenirs from our travels: a ceramic bowl decorated in snails, a stone from the mountains, a plant in a fabric basket.

When we were finished, we both sat down on the couch and put up our feet on the edge of the table.

It was something we'd wanted for a long time.

To have a table in the living room where we could rest our legs.

I looked at Ciro, smiled and leaned over against his shoulder. Suddenly, I felt his body stiffen.

I moved away. I tried to make eye contact with him again, but he wouldn't look at me. Something had darkened the air.

Are you okay? I asked.

I love you, but I just can't take it anymore, he said.

Understanding it would surely bring some relief: a logical chain of actions, a story, something that would lead us to a climax, a confrontation, a crisis, a narrative, in which the characters' motivations are clear.

That's what's missing. That's what isn't there. There's nothing to get us to the third act. No point of inflection that might explain it.

That night, at dawn, I got up, went down the stairs. The house was dark. Ciro wasn't asleep, I could hear him tossing and turning on the couch.

I can't believe this is actually happening, I said, standing there, halfway down, on one of the middle steps. I can't believe a relationship like ours could end the same way as some adolescent romance, I said. I can't believe there's no way to reverse it, to talk about it, to give it another chance.

Ciro turned ever so slightly on the couch, lifting his head a little. How could you not see it. How could you not see the signs, he said.

What signs? When? What did you say that I didn't hear? This afternoon we went to buy a table together. Yesterday we spent four hours looking at tables on Mercado Libre together.

Ciro didn't say anything. In the dim light, I couldn't see his face.

Then he said, I've already gone through this. I've already grieved.

During the first months, I told everyone that Ciro had left me, that I had no idea why, that it had been a sudden decision, that he had asked me to leave the house – our house – that that night he had slept on the couch, and that the following morning, he had asked me again:

Seriously, please, get out, I can't do this anymore. Get out. Now.

We didn't end. He ended us.

I needed to say it that way. I couldn't talk about it otherwise. I was so ashamed of also having been responsible, of disregarding, of not giving space.

That tormented me, because that refusal to see made me guilty, too.

The messages at all hours of the night, the messages that said, How's it going? or, What are you up to? that actually meant, Want to talk? Want to get back together? The messages he left unanswered.

The early mornings thinking what I'd say to him, why, to what end.

All the emails I wrote and didn't send.

'There's no one less desirable than a person you have ceased to desire.'

That's what I am to Ciro, someone he stopped wanting.

Sometimes I feel like I'll never understand what happened with us. And that if I did understand it, the painful part would be over, and I could leave this all behind.

Sometimes I feel like I do understand it, like I understand it perfectly, but it still hurts.

And sometimes I think that there are things you never fully understand, things that linger, hovering around us, ready to attack at any moment.

That the painful part is never really over, that it only retreats for a few hours, a few days, and then it takes you by surprise, floods you, knocks you off your feet, and that you have to learn to live with that.

How do you write a pained body?
How does a pained body write?

Now it's hot inside the house, too. It's even hot at night. There's nothing I can do about it. It's Tuesday and, according to the forecast, these temperatures will last till Friday. All I can do is wait. The sun scorches everything in the vegetable garden, in the fields. It overwhelms, it makes my chest tight. I don't have a fan. Things are roasting, the silence is colossal, everything is very white. It's almost six in the evening, and it's sweltering. The baked earth, the naked earth, the earth that splits into fissures. Nature doesn't shelter. These days, Zapiola isn't a place that keeps safe, that nourishes. Zapiola has transformed, and now it's harsh, and it's endlessly demanding. Nature doesn't relent, it tortures.

Drought and the plains. Nature wins. You can't fight it. You have to surrender to its volatility. Surrender to whatever the days bring. Sometimes the countryside feels like a punishment, like steps backward. It only sparks negligence, neglect.

I go into town to buy some meat. Brick cutters working in full sunlight. On each side, a backhoe that bellows as it excavates, its arms scraping over and over the bottom of the wells, sending up huge clods, immense shovelfuls of earth.

They've lit a kiln, and the plumes of smoke from the big block of burning adobe rise into a dark stain, between grey and dirty white, that unfolds like a fan across a sky that is too blue, without a single cloud.

On the way back, I run into Luiso, riding his bike from his house.

Think it'll rain? I ask, pointing to some clouds to the north.

Nah. The sun went down neat.

What about there? I say and signal some even smaller clouds, to the south.

Could be, we'll just have to see if it'll build. They look like they could rain in the early morning, Luiso says.

But it's just a fifteen percent chance, I answer, having taken advantage of getting reception in the town and checked the forecast on my phone.

It's not going to rain a drop, I think to myself.

We have to be patient, says Luiso. Maybe, with a little luck…

We'll see, I say.

We'll see, he says.

In the end, it doesn't rain.

It's cloudy in the morning. The cool air makes me want to do things again. I sowed a few rows of radishes, deep, an inch or so in, we'll see if I'll get to harvest any this way (the moon is a waning crescent, they should at least sprout). I also planted cress and transplanted more chard. I protected the new plantings with plastic mesh and the chard with bottles cut to cover them with partial shade. I planted a row of leeks and another of beets. I put in wicker posts, arching them, driving them down into the ground, and I find that they are perfect for sustaining partial shade. At ten, the sky has cleared completely, and the sun is becoming oppressive. I begin to grow embittered again. There are still six or seven hours of extreme heat, of birds lurking, of ants, of dryness.

I still haven't learned how to surrender to the rhythms and the misadventures of the garden.

Outside only the snakes and iguanas are active. The radishes and the arugula are barely surviving in their partial shade. The same goes for the transplanted chard, protected by bottles. I also covered the leek and beetroot seedlings with partial shade, but I have a suspicion they won't sprout regardless. The only thing that's looking more or less okay is the peppers. The squash is languid, worn out. The green beans and the tomatoes seem to be at a standstill.

The grass is dry, the thistles are dry, the weeds along the road are dry. Everything is dry and static, on the verge of burning, on the verge of cracking apart.

To keep calm, to be patient. This heat, these heatwaves, will pass, and there are peaceful days, beautiful days to come.

I was planning to start writing a story, one of the ones the separation put on hold, but in the end, inertia won, the *what's the point* won, the *who cares*. I sat down, reread a couple of paragraphs, and thought: Who were these characters? Why did I find them interesting? Why would I ever have cared about their stories? What could have made me think I needed to sit down and tell them? That was another life. Scraps of another life.

Extreme heat. A white squall on the horizon, but no sign of it arriving yet. Lethargy and silence all afternoon. The crossbeams sway. The roof creaks.

The air pressure has dropped.

When I wake up again, the storm has taken hold of the whole sky overhead. Heavy clouds, dark blue, purplish, greenish, in certain regions almost black. So much silence and above, very high up, above even the clouds, thunder like a distant rearrangement of furniture.

If we get any precipitation, I think, it's going to be hail.

I pull out a deck chair and sit under the eucalyptus trees to watch the countryside, the dried-up marshland in the distance, a little grove of black acacias and silver poplars almost as far away as I can see, the poplar leaves fluttering against the ominous backdrop of the sky.

There is an explosion of little birds, I have no idea where they came from. They're about the size of sparrows, and they look similar to sparrows, but they're not sparrows. It's a massive flock. They fly in circles, in Ss, describing irregular patterns in the air. From the branches of the eucalyptus, hundreds take off simultaneously, moving into the darkness over the field, somersaulting, gliding, chirping, zigzagging, drawing figure eights and circles and tight curves, then loose ones, in the sky. A great confusion of small birds that then, almost all at the exact same time, vacate the sky and go back to sitting on the highest branches overhead. Again and again: excursions into the hot air that immediately precedes the storm, as though they are performing some ritual dance, sketching out a spell, tracing in the air an incantation with the unpredictable trajectories of their flights.

Is it a ceremony to protect us from the hail? To bring about the rain? To keep it from raining?

After a while, the birds calm down, the storm moves on to the east. The sky is grey and heavy, low clouds, humid heat. It no longer seems possible that so much as five millimetres of rain will fall.

You can't control a vegetable garden, and that exasperates me sometimes. A garden cannot grow out of my desire, but rather on its own power, the power of its seeds, and all its growth occurs in the midst of accidents.

Writing is similar: I used to write, at times, under the illusion that I was in control of the text, when in reality everything kept happening in a manner that almost excluded me: whatever could sprout did so in the midst of my own accidents, my neurosis, my tiredness, my lethargy, my fear of what people might say, and would they be bored, and what will they think of me, my fear that nobody would like it, that they'd put down the book halfway through without picking it back up. Such slips are not so different from drought, or wind, or hail. They attack the seed. Stories grow in their midst, modelled and marred by me. Sometimes they don't survive. Other times I give them nothing. Some stories I can't help along, I don't know how to write them.

Being with another person is hard. Being with another person is work, effort. Understanding, or not understanding, or trying to understand. What you think you are. What the other person thinks you are. Your wants and needs. What the other person wants. What the other person needs. The other person's work and your work. Teamwork: work, the relationship, the friendship, the proximity. Wear, misunderstandings, doubts. What isn't seen, what isn't heard, what you don't want to see, what is so excruciatingly painful you would rather not know.

Did I decide to write because it's something I can do by myself? Because I can control whatever happens inside the world of the story, in that little universe?

Plot and suspense as a way to entertain, a way to be entertaining. A way of being with someone else but not allowing them to speak, not listening to them, not making the effort of trying to understand them.

I've already gone through this, said Ciro. I've already grieved. He closed the book. He set it down. He decided not to pick it up again.

'People make things – make art or things that are akin to art – as a way of expressing their need for contact, or their fear of it,' I read, enveloped by afternoon heat, in a book by Olivia Laing.

To give in to whatever nature decides. Its rhythms, the weather, the drought. At nine in the morning, it is already thirty-five degrees.

Subdued by the heat. A couple of times I go out to hose myself down in the cold water from the pump. A dazed mockingbird comes up, hopping aimlessly through the grass, mouthing something with its head tilted back, beak open in a V, as though pleading with the sky. I have the feeling the bird will drop dead at any moment. Slowly, trying not to scare it, I turn on the hose, letting the water run so that it forms a puddle in the grass. The mockingbird stays a while, sitting on the wet lawn, as if it's incubating. Then it pecks, digs at the ground. After a while, it takes off.

Luiso tells me that in town, on account of the heat, one woman lost eighteen of her chickens. Another, whose coop is in direct sun, released all her chickens onto the square so they could go under plants and seek their own cool. It'll be a long time before she can gather them up again, but at least they didn't die on her.

And a man who breeds rabbits had to spend the whole afternoon throwing buckets of water over the roofs of the rabbit hutches, but he did save them. Only one of them died, and it was sickly anyway.

The sun going down like a perfect orange disk, enormous, in back of the yellow grassland. In spite of the heat, in the calm of the evening, the landscape looks beautiful to me. The same landscape for all time: the same landscape for the Pampa people and the Rankülche, for the colonizers, for William Henry Hudson and his family of Englishmen lost in South America, for those who laid the railroads, for the Italian and Basque immigrants, for those who built the chapel and planted the trees on the square, for those who installed a milking yard in the forties and those who melted it down in the seventies, for those who came here to hide out during the dictatorship, for those who bought weekend houses here in an effort to save their children from cement.

The same landscape, always. The grassland rises, stretches, fruits in spikes, falls, dies, is born again out of seeds. Nature always identical to itself. Plains for miles and miles. Plains for decades and decades. Plains for centuries, for millennia.

What am I doing here alone? What's going to happen now? What am I doing with my life? I boil some green beans and start looking over the sowing calendar. The house is neat and clean, it's an oppressive night, there's no breeze, no cooling. The calendar and my plans (picturing new beds in the garden, new gardens, fresh futures, so many pipe dreams) distract me, and my heartsickness passes.

Different ways of saying this in different languages.

How the English-speaking say *killing time*. The abyss between *passing* the time and *killing* it.

The way the English-speaking distinguish between solitude and loneliness, with two different words.

I finish dinner and hear some noises outside. I go up to the window, and I see the lights of the truck that belongs to the neighbour who keeps pigs as they get smaller and smaller down the road. Now I really am completely alone in the countryside. Now my malaise returns, my discomfort. I even feel fear. It's hot, my sheets are sticky. I can't sleep with the window open. I think how someone could come in, club me, beat me. Who would hear my screams? I barely sleep, as any noise from outside, any creak of the furniture or popping of the metal sheets on the roof as they expand immediately wakes me up and puts me on edge. Until at half past three in the morning, it starts to shimmer out behind the eucalyptus.

Half an hour later, the storm finally comes, and it cools down. At first it looks like it's going to be just a quick little cloudburst, but then the rain grows gentle and even.

Now it's half past eight, and it's still raining. Relief. The grass regreens before my eyes. I make myself some coffee.

Luiso is in the shed, with the radio on. Last night around eleven the moon was already indicating moisture, he tells me.

What do you mean?

When the moon has a mist around it, a halo, that's it indicating moisture, he explains.

Now it's cool and raining. It's raining slowly in the blue morning. The leaves of the tree shine like they're varnished, and, soaked in water, colours intensify.

It's still raining.

It's raining calmly, a fine mist.

MARCH

The wood stove, the Tupperware with sausage and cheeses on the granite counter, the pitcher of fresh milk. The smell of burnt coffee. Breakfast. Uncle Tonito's canvas sandals sliding across the floor. The green tiles with white stripes, stripes with waves, like zebras have, but worn, discoloured by years and years of particular routes repeated. The crate of firewood. My grandfather's smile.

What are you doing up already? he asks instead of saying good morning.

My grandma is still in bed. Grandpa comes and goes via the hallway, from the kitchen to the bedroom, brewing her three or four mates before she gets up. She drinks them on her side, leaning on one arm, in her nightgown, her hair at times a chaos, at other times flattened by sleep. Her face swollen, the remains of the night in her eyes, on her cheeks, in the folds of her wrinkles.

As soon as they're dressed, they make the beds. On opposite sides of their big bed: between the bed and the window, my grandpa; between the bed and the wardrobe, Grandma. The sheets undulate in the air, reflected in the dresser mirror, expanding. With her hand on the mattress, her palm gliding, my grandma smooths them fast. One blanket, then the other, fluffing the pillows, unfolding the bedspread so that it falls to either side, the same length on either side, so that it's even.

Uncle Tonito goes for a drive in the old light blue Ford. I sit in the passenger's seat. A few dogs in the back, in the bed of the truck. Others running alongside the wheels. Cacique, when I was very young. A collie that looked like Lassie, but haughty, tricky. Once he bit my leg. And then, further ahead, Colita and Manchita, mutts, mongrels, little ratters found along the roads.

Uncle Tonito drives very slowly, the dogs have time to entertain themselves with armadillo burrows, with wild hares, with partridges that skim the ground as they fly. We follow the wire fences. We make sure none of the wires has been cut in the night, that no cow or calf has escaped. I don't know if this is strictly necessary, or just a way to pass the time. Uncle Tonito doesn't talk. We drive through the countryside in silence, each of us lost in thought. I don't know what Uncle Tonito is looking at in the furrows, in the vegetation, in the cows, what changes he identifies, those small alterations, movements. I don't pay much attention. The meaning of these rounds escapes me. It doesn't even occur to me that there could be a reason why behind them. For me it's no more than a ritual, a meaningless routine. Something you just do, every day.

Sometimes the dogs bark. At no point in all the years I can remember was there ever a cow missing, a severed wire, a downed post.

Bumps in the road, little jolts of the truck as it goes over ruts, clods of earth, trembling of windowpanes, and in the sheet metal floor, a clod of earth glimpsed through a gap. The owls that watch us from the posts they stand on, turning their heads in order to follow our movements. Between husks of corn, a run of mice. The shadows of the chimangos darkening the sky.

Later, when we're back, we drink a couple of mates by the wood-burning stove, and then there is the second morning task: walking around the chicken coops in the grove, clutching the handle of a bucket where I am supposed to collect the fresh eggs.

It is like a treasure hunt. Uncle Tonito gives me my instructions: bend down, look carefully under the box of the seed drill, slip in through the cane field and search up against the fence, peek into the open trunk of an old chinaberry tree, into the burned interior of a eucalyptus – they always lay there, there's a nest toward the back – climb up to the mill and look under the pump, or behind the woodpile, or among the bales, or the rolls of old wire.

And returning in triumph, from the mill, from the chinaberry tree, from the eucalyptus, holding a warm egg.

Little by little, the bucket fills up.

The real heat is behind us now, summer's letting up. The shift is almost imperceptible, but summer is abating. Now it is seeding season. Thistledown floats in the air, carried far away, scattering, coming apart.

My grandfather used to call the dandelions bakers. I liked to blow those little fluff bombs furiously, until they completely fell apart and drifted off.

Fall is coming, now will be the most beautiful season for the garden. The light has already changed, and only in the afternoons is it still too white and too strong, a light that is reflected in the ground and forces you to squint, shrinking your pupils.

Beautiful day. Cool and humid after the rain. In the afternoon, I go into town on my bike. On the way there, I take the back road, the one with the abandoned house and the rectangle of forest. On the way back, I pass by the brick kilns, taking the main road as far as the chicken farm, and then the local road, narrow and covered in weeds, that leads straight to my house. The tyre tracks of the cars that went by this morning set in the wet mud of the road. The tracks of the tractor a dairy farmer used to pull a milk trailer are almost ditches. Lots of puddles and a light layer of mud that has stuck to the wheels of my bike and made forward movement slow, difficult.

One of the round squashes I planted in January has already formed its first fruits. They're the size of a china-berry, but they're growing.

The wind picks up just a little. A great kiskadee is using the cows' drinking trough as a washbasin. At first it skims the water, still in flight, but then it dives all the way in. Standing on a post, it shakes out its feathers. With its beak, it rearranges them, spruces itself up.

I'm pulling the second crop of radishes, to throw them out, because they've all done poorly, and I want to plant lettuce in that bed, when I encounter a surprise. Under a red ribbed root that had protruded about two inches out of the ground, there is a little radish bulb. Immediately I pull more and more. In the end, from a bed I'd written off as a total loss, almost half of the plants had grown bulbs. Twenty radishes in a bowl renew my hope and my desire to do things in the garden. Spicy little radishes. Summer radishes, fed with water from the hose. Drought radishes.

The green beans I planted and prepared such tall supports for, with canes and wire, so that they could climb as they liked, turned out to be dwarf beans. I was worried because they weren't really growing, and today I saw that they were already in full flower, some of them had already sprung their little beans. I must have mixed up the seed packets. The plants are short, they don't even reach up to my knees, but it seems like they're going to produce a significant yield. While the supports, those strange structures, canes stuck into the ground like inverted Vs, like tepee poles, right in the middle of the vegetable garden, were erected altogether in vain.

The cool, diaphanous air of a sunset after a stormy day.
A glorious sunset, amazing vistas, fans of white clouds, almost like spirals dissolving between orange and light blue, cool weather.

Each day here begins with the neighbour starting the tractor, at half past six in the morning, to go and feed the pigs, and with the racket of the chickens at the farm, far away, on the corner of the main road. It's a dull, remote racket, more like a burbling, like the sea with seagulls, and gradually it dies down, until only the shrieks of the chimangos and the southern lapwings remain. On windy days, it's not audible at all. It took me a while to realize it was chickens. Now I think that at that time someone must raise the curtains that cover, on both sides, the long sheds filled with cages. And that, with the sudden light, the chickens wake up and start clucking. Or maybe it's just that they're fed at that time. The farm is a mystery to me. It's the only moment of the day when the chickens can be heard. They're white chickens, broilers, fat. If I walk past them I can barely make them out behind a row of casuarinas. Sometimes white feathers turn up against the fence of the vegetable garden, as though the wind had whipped them up and left them stuck there, like gifts, like offerings.

Luiso arrives at seven, I can see him from a long way away, coming up the road on his bicycle. I make myself some coffee and take my cup out to the garden. We chat a while. He tells me the latest from the town, what's being said about the weather. I ask his opinion on the ants, on the lettuce.

I take advantage of the cool in the air and spend the first few hours of the day out working in the garden. Yesterday I created a new bed, with a border around it made out of old tiles. I put compost and sand in it so that the soil would be very loose, and I planted carrots and garlic and a little spinach there. I wonder how they'll do. It was a peaceful morning, with a beautiful sun that wasn't quite hot. There was no wind. Silence. I transplanted all the aromatics to the new bed. The cabbages and kales came up perfect, and they're already sticking out almost half an inch over the edges of their trays. The broccoli and the cauliflower, too. The chicory I planted before the rain came up sparse, and soon after its emergence, the ants ate it all again. Next time, I'll try planting it in a furrow.

I eat whatever I have lying around for lunch, standing, over the stove. I eat straight from the pot and let the dirty dishes and glasses accumulate in the sink, washing them once a week, at the most. In the afternoons, I try to nap. Sometimes I spend a while on my computer, going through old files. If not, I read, go for a walk, or go back into the garden.

Today I sowed delphiniums and calendulas in the new plot. I also transplanted the chard and the stunted lettuce plants that survived the dry period and sowed some more lettuce directly in the ground, between the two furrows of garlic. It's not so hot anymore, so I've decided that from now on, I'm going to stop planting the lettuce plants in plugs and start sowing them in rows, nice and dense, to thin it out later. I'll get to eat the smaller ones as baby lettuce, and in doing so, I'll be making room for the ones that remain, so that they grow wide, spread out.

When I had finished the lettuce, I turned on the water heater and took a very hot bath. Then I set up the deck chair under the eucalyptus trees and watched the sky change on the horizon: from light blue to purple, to orange, to turquoise. Later, from below, a band of another blue, a dull cerulean, almost the colour of night. The eucalyptus leaves were very still. The only audible thing was the parrots screaming sometimes, settling into their nests, and when the parrots finally fell silent, the extended shrieks of the chimangos, calling to each other as they glided over my head.

The humidity of the rain lingers in the permeated earth and rises from the field, and I could feel it, in my arms, in my face, in my legs. The cool air swelled my lungs, grazed my cheeks.

In the end, to the west, there was a band of pale orange, a glow, but by then I could no longer distinguish between things, the trees and their branches had turned into one black mass that barely contrasted with the darkening blue to the east.

I got cold then, and went inside the house.
The deck chair slept outside.

News of the day: outside, on the road, the pampas grass has blossomed. Their white crests in the wind, moving just barely.

When the food was ready, I was in charge of setting the table and running to call Grandpa and Uncle Tonito for lunch. We always sat in the same spots. Uncle Tonito at the head, Grandma and Grandpa facing each other. Me next to Grandpa. Uncle Tonito would make a few comments about the fields. Grandpa would nod in agreement, and Grandma would recount something she had heard that morning on the radio. They spoke in Piedmontese when they talked about adult things and didn't want me to understand.

I wasn't curious about their conversations, I didn't even pay attention to them. When they switched to Piedmontese, I would sit still, silent, cutting my meat or chicken into smaller and smaller pieces, pondering something, coming up with little stories to tell myself.
Time passed without my growing restless.
I don't know what I did with time then. I don't remember.

I'd gather up the tablecloth, go shake it outside, put the chairs upside down against the table.
Grandma would wash the dishes, Grandpa would dry them, and my job was to sweep the floor.
White vinyl chairs. Gold rings on their black metal legs.

Sweeping in the same order always, starting from the pantry, moving toward the centre. Beginning again from the front door, moving, again, toward the centre. Sweeping under the folding chairs that served as lounge chairs, sweeping under the window with the mosquito net and green curtains, sweeping under the stove. Moving the crate of firewood, sweeping, putting it back where it was.

The little mound of trash our steps had generated over the course of the morning on the green and white floor, with its undulating, zebra-like stripes.

The full pantry, the high shelf over the sewing machine. The dusters that hung from the coat rack. The feather duster, the dust wands, the dusters made out of scraps. The green Siam fridge. The mosquito net. Strips of plastic curtain billowing in the doorway. The ironstone brick to keep the door open, like a kind of pedestal or plinth, with a big crack in it and some other smaller ones, worn and torn by time.

While my grandma mopped the floor, I had to take the trash out to the chickens. The midday sun suffusing the immensity of the quinta. The onion bed. The lilies where the washing machine drained. The purple arrowroot. The agave. The plum trees. Unruly string beans, climbing up the cane supports, up the fence, up the rose bushes. Iron frames with wire mesh to protect the chicory, the lettuce from the birds. The garlic. The pear and peach trees, the rosemary, the whitebrush, the lemon verbena, the pomegranate plant, the giant laurel, its leaves always blackened, sticky, coated in dirt. A ton of broadcast chard in winter. A bushy fennel. In the summer, watermelon and a gigantic squash field that ranged from green to yellow. The cats that were always giving birth to gruff little kittens in the shade of their large leaves that looked like berets, like hat brims.

Tossing the contents of the trash can over the wire mesh. The chickens coming running without needing to be called. Potato skins, eggshells, halved lemons, squeezed, bones from cutlets, bones from stew, a long orange peel that twisted, curled. Chickens digging among the corn silk, cluck-clucking, looking out of one eye, looking out of the other, searching for treasures with their beaks. The beating of their nervous hearts reflected in their necks. Their blunt bright red crests, just a little droopy, tilted to one side.

The only Piedmontese words I ever learned (I don't really know how to spell them, just know how I heard them pronounced):

Engambará
Sgonfiar
Sbranar
Fía
Cien
Fioca (Ñoca)
Girín
Brundular
Vichoca, bachoca
Fiap
Magún
Babacio
Bunumas
Andoma (Anduma)
Fafujiar/furfuiar
Badòla

Yesterday I went to Lobos and bought four chicks. They're ordinary layers, I wanted scrappier cross-bred chickens and asked around, but nobody in the town has those these days. I had no choice but to buy layers at the seed farm. They're already quite big, the salesman told me that in two months they'll reach the 'point of lay'. Once they've reached it, you have to stop giving them baby chick food and start them on a blend designed for layers.

Lots of people start giving that to them earlier, to speed them up, but that'll ruin the animals, the salesman explained to me.

These chickens are genetically modified, he told me. They won't brood, but you can turn a rooster loose on them, and the eggs will come out fine, whereas if you turn him onto a different type of chicken you'll get chicks.

I brought my four chickens back in a box. By the time I got home, it was noon already. I put the chickens in a little room inside the coop, had something to eat and lay down to take a nap. At some point, half asleep, I thought I heard a commotion outside. At first, I figured it would be the shrieks of the chimangos as they crested the wind, but then I woke up all the way and realized it was the chicks.

I ran to see what was happening. The big iguana had got into the chicken coop and cornered the chicks against the sheet metal. The iguana was swishing its tail like a crocodile, and the chicks, terrified, were clambering over one another, chirping desperately in a frenzy of feathers and flaps. I looked around for a stick, but as soon as it saw me, the iguana clambered up the sheet metal and slipped through a hole at about the height of my knee and scurried across the grass. Its run was prehistoric, a clumsy sprint, tail zigzagging, lightning fast this way and that. I chased it as it approached the woodpile at full speed, but it was faster, it got there first, and then there was no way to find it again or to make it come out.

I don't know if it wanted to eat the chicks or if it was looking for eggs. I put the little hens in another box and brought them inside the house. That night, they'd sleep with me.

I covered the hole the iguana had come in through with an extra sheet of metal. I released the chicks back into the coop, and they seem to be fine. Nonetheless, I continue to feel uneasy. Working in the garden, I go back every ten minutes to check on them, make sure nothing is wrong. At siesta hour, I barely sleep. My ear attuned to any noise at all times.

Very early in the morning the dew reveals the fine cobwebs between the clovers and the blades of Bermuda grass that surround the squashes. They are like snippets of intricate gauze.

The squashes do not bear fruit, they flower a lot but don't fruit. The weeds have vanquished them and surround them and are closing in on them, and their flowers emerge pointing upwards. It's cloudy.

The beets came up very unevenly, the parsley won't sprout, the cilantro is scraggly, the arugula is covered in white pustules on the underside of its leaves, out of the entire potato bed, only one potato sprouted, and the chard was eaten up by birds. I anguish over all of it, despair.

I wish everything were simpler, I wish I could bring home some chickens and have them just lay eggs. I wish

I could scatter some seeds and have them all sprout, have the vegetable beds all come out perfectly, not face any setbacks.

But no, I have to wait for the hens to mature, have to protect them from the iguana, from the weasel, pray they will survive, wait two, three months, who knows how long exactly. I have to get used to the fact that half of what you sow won't happen, have to get used to it not raining, to the plants getting sick, to insects.

I try to fumigate the squashes with diatomaceous earth solution, but the nozzle gets clogged, once, twice, three times. I hate them, I hate the squashes, I hate the nozzle. Life becomes hard, dark. Everything goes wrong, everything is shit. I dump the solution all over them now, screw the squashes, they can do whatever they want, let the stupid green bugs feast upon them.

I get mad at the plants, as though they were doing this to me on purpose, as though they were to blame.

Lots of little things that put me in a foul mood. The world is made up of setbacks and things that don't work and failures in the garden and regrets.

Why can't I just be content, just by virtue of being here, just by virtue of having a garden? So the ants eat all the chard, who cares, it didn't work out this time, but I'll plant it again, there will be other seasons, I'm only starting out…

No. I want everything right now. Everything this minute. Everything grown. Everything perfect. For what? For whom?

I know I need to calm down. I need to calm down.

'People blame one for dwelling on trivialities, but life

is made up of them,' says Barbara Pym in an interview I read yesterday.

The answer isn't, of course, 'this shit isn't going to get me down,' nor is it 'everything is a disaster and nothing ever goes right,' but rather something along the lines of, 'patience, it's my first time, I'm learning, there will be other gardens, this drought will pass, etcetera, etcetera, etcetera.'

Patience, patience. This will pass. Patience.
I should tattoo it on the back of my hand so as not to forget.

There are things that do go right: the dwarf beans produce and produce and keep on flowering. I harvest them every day, by the fistful. Two days' harvest makes for a good salad with hard-boiled eggs. The tomato continues to grow and flower more, and there are now some ripe little tomatoes. Yesterday I cut off two, and there are two more for tomorrow. And for next week there is another truss that's looking promising.

'The house is so much like me it's like talking to myself, and my own company bores me,' I read in a book about Cy Twombly.

Does this house in Zapiola resemble me? It's an old house, from the thirties or forties. It has a dark kitchen that faces east and gets next to no sunlight, only a little very early in the morning. A living room of sorts, or a receiving area, with a stove for heating, a window with a partition that divides the glass, a French window that faces the road. Two bedrooms. The room on the south side is the coolest and most humid one in the house.

The other room, where I put my desk and my whole library, receives the afternoon sun from the siesta hour until sunset. That's where I'm supposed to be writing a short story at this precise instant, and instead, here I am, sprawled out on the couch, rapidly scribbling these notes in my notebook.

The first time I entered this house, the feeling I had was of walking into some great-aunt's home. A cosy, welcoming space. The most beautiful thing about it is the floors in the kitchen and the living room: limestone that forms rhomboid patterns, in brown and ochre tones, a direct link to the floors of houses from my childhood that were already relics then. As for the rest, like any old house, the foundations do not have an insulating layer, moisture rises from the ground up the walls, yellow stains that gradually expand into white, peeling plaster, debris that falls next to the loose skirting boards.

I walk through the house from one room to another and my mind ping-pongs, coiling in on itself, always thinking the same things, dwelling on the same mistakes, the same regrets, what I could have done so that everything would now be different, etcetera, etcetera, etcetera.

'A too-solitary animal ends up eating itself,' says Sara Gallardo.

At times I feel I need to see people, but who would water the garden if I flit off to Buenos Aires? Who would feed the chickens? Who would get rid of the ants? Who would shoo away the birds in the afternoons? And besides, I can't go to Buenos Aires. Who would I want to see? The terror of running into Ciro on whatever random corner, having one of my friends tell me they ran into him in this or that café, that he's seeing someone, that they saw him talking to some guy.

It isn't easy being alone. Or going back to being alone. It's yet another thing I need to learn how to do.

Digging, loosening the topsoil, pulling weeds, creating furrows, shoving wheelbarrows of earth from one place to another, looking for branches to protect what's been planted, putting up nets, going out into the cane field to cut canes. Watering, watering, swinging the hose back and forth. Loosening the topsoil again, digging again, creating another bed. All is solved by doing.

Late last night, or in the very early morning, something outside woke me up. The noise of sheet metal, of movement. A weasel in the henhouse, I thought. I went to check it out with my flashlight and found nothing. The chicks just sleeping on the ground, their necks pulled in between their wings, all pressed into one corner, huddled close as if they were cold. It's been several days since I gave them some sticks so they could go and sleep higher up, but either they still can't fly or they still haven't figured out how yet.

I went back to bed, but I wasn't sleepy anymore. A thousand thoughts were running through my head. In the silence of the night, the refrigerator motor. I couldn't relax and ignore it. Tiredness and the need not to focus.

I fell asleep very late and woke up very late. Now it's nine o'clock, I've already had two cups of coffee, and I still can't shake the drowsiness from my body. Lethargy. No desire to work. Outside it's a cool, clear morning, but now a little southerly wind has picked up again, and the sky is clouding back over.

I inspect the garden. Slow but sure, the zinnias are about to bloom. They'll last until the first frost. It's something. The squashes are beautiful, they continue to fruit and grow, stretching out. The leeks, the pincushion flowers, the rue and the chives that I transplanted the other day to the new bed seem to have taken, with no real issues. In the plug tray, oxheart cabbage and Red Russian kale grow strong. The lettuce plants have come up, too. I tie the new shoots of the Chinese tomato plant to the stakes and the smell of them stays on my hands. It's one of my favourite smells in the whole world.

I transplant the cabbages into individual pots and finish setting up the new bed. In the large bed, where there used to be potatoes that were never successful, I plant broad beans and peas. I harvest the third batch of radishes. Much better than the first batch, but, like the second, only half formed a bulb. I still suspect it's because they didn't get enough sun, so they stretched out in the hopes of better light.

In the bed with the tiles around it, the garlic is starting to sprout. The spinach came up nice and even.

The Chinese tomato plant keeps giving and giving. Dwarf beans in copious harvests.

South wind all day. It was like this from the start, barely calming down in the afternoon and still blowing now, as the day is ending. It's been cool, but sunny. Yesterday's humidity is mostly gone. Wind wailing between the trees.

I go out for a bike ride, up to the town, by the road with the forest rectangle, and, on the way back, by the main road. The brickmakers dismantling a kiln, loading a truck with tall towers of bricks. Beautiful greyish sunset, now it does seem like a fall day. Coming back, against the wind, my bike was heavy. And yet, that sensation of freedom, of open space, of air in your face, of a cool wind and the leaden blue sky and the sun flaming orange. A pleasant tiredness. The pampas' breadth.

Sometimes I get lost. I forget that I'm this now. Walking slowly along the back road, the overgrown, high road, that no one else uses ever. Going for a walk at sunset on a beautiful evening. The noises of all the birds in the marsh. Bugs that move between the weeds. Silence.

When I manage to get out of the buzz buzz of my head and my obsession with the success of the garden, when I manage to look around – at the distant horizon, at the clouds, at how the vegetation on the road is changing – Zapiola is calm. Something about its outside gets reflected in my inside. Something in me starts dissolving. A cool little breeze. A sun that isn't especially bothersome now. Birdsong. Stillness. Something about all this is soothing to me.

I have to let the countryside fill me and teach me.
I have to learn to watch and not try to impose my will.

Living in the middle of nowhere is also a bit claustrophobic. In a town or a city you can go out, see other people, interact, forget your problems for a little while or even just meet up with someone to discuss your problems with, get a little relief. Here you're alone in the landscape.
Landscape as mirror. Through all the bad and all the good.
To give yourself time.

Only horizon all around. And, from time to time,

that straight line interrupted by a hill of trees, eucalyptus, chinaberry trees, and poplars for firewood. Elms, acacias, the occasional palm.

Like when you draw a line with drawing ink and an old nib, and the ink runs, thickens into lumps, little perturbations, mistakes by what is trying to be horizontal, flat, perfect: distant hills/mills/mounds/places where people live.

A tall tumult of eucalyptus trees, a crescent of cypresses and casuarinas, a belt of thick cane clinging to the back of the hill of the trees that are for firewood, the wheel of a mill that looms.

The cane fields act as a wall, turn the farmhouse into a sort of fortress. Past the cane fields: empty lots and open pampa. And on this side of them, a safe space where houses, sheds, and chicken coops coexist, old ploughs that rust under the chinaberry trees, loose hens that scrabble and build little nests, wild fruit trees, the vegetable garden, agaves, the garbage pit, sheds, the tank, some silos. A refuge, its routines.

The siesta hour used to always be my hour of freedom. The rest of the time there was always some adult around, keeping an eye on me, making me do things, but in the siesta, with my grandparents asleep and the house kept dark, closed to keep in the cool, all I had to do was stand on the bed, lift the roller shade, very slowly, praying it wouldn't make any noise, and, having opened it, hop outside.

I was never mischievous, never did anything out of the ordinary, I was just a very quiet, near-sighted child who spent his time inspecting things too closely. I would go through that world contained within the crescent of cane fields as if it were an abandoned amusement park: I'd peek into the water tank to see if any toads had fallen inside; I'd jump in between the ploughs and seeders abandoned at the base of the hill – splatters of greyish, copper, and aquamarine lichens like welts on the dull, rusted tools that had been there for decades, weeds growing in between shuttles and bars – and one by one I'd reinspect the nests in the chicken coops Uncle Tonito had taken me to check in the morning; I'd search among the bags of ground corn in the hopes of coming across a litter of mice; I'd climb up into the space between stockades and try to open and close the two big wood eaves that made up the trap to the cattle chute.

I'd stroll around the sheds, the garage: from the walls and the ceiling hung incomprehensible iron shapes, boxes, spare parts, rubber rings, springs, tyres, jars filled with nuts and screws and washers. Everything was vaguely mysterious, attractive. I liked to play alone among those forgotten things that were covered in dirt, objects accumulated in basements, in sheds, in the junk room, pressed up against the peeling walls, in piles. I liked spending time there, investigating, imagining what they once were, what they were used for, who had been their owners, what stories they concealed.

I associated the external world with being bored. Back then, in the afternoons, after the siesta, when my grandparents got up, I had to work in the confined space of the garden, loosening the topsoil, pulling weeds from in between the lettuce and the chard, transplanting onions or leeks, with my grandmother, both of us on our knees, in the dirt. At times, I could hear the distant roar of the tractors in the fields, of the cows that would low at their watering holes, but in general, the realms beyond the cane fields and the cypresses didn't interest me. Excursions out were with Uncle Tonito, never solo. And it wasn't so much the external world that intrigued me, but rather the going with him, the speed of the truck, the landscape moving, passing by slowly. That sort of infinity into which the horizon, seen from the truck window, transforms. The procession of fields and narrow passageways, getting out to open and close gates, calling dogs, watching them slurp water from the troughs.

I don't remember exactly when my tastes changed. I don't remember exactly when I started going out on my own. Maybe it was merely the passage of time. Maybe it was coming to understand that the plains had to do with growing, with no longer being a child.

The day I discovered the pleasure of going out past the cane fields and walking alone across the open countryside.

In the winter at dusk, as my grandmother ironed atop a blanket laid over one end of the kitchen table, I would leave the cane fields behind, advance along the dead-end track, jump over the wire fence and concentrate on walking through the deep green fields of oats. Looking across the field, the blue-green of the oats contrasting with the low clouds in the leaden sky. The wind in my face, eyes lost on the horizon. I'd squint to avoid crossed lines. I was outside the walls and *by myself,* as people say in English. A way of being in yourself. Me in the landscape. Me on the plain. Single-handed but in touch.

It was a space where I could find myself.
It was a place where I could read myself.

The beginning of a conversation with the landscape.

On the horizon, between the marsh and the small hill of silver poplars, a layer of white fog has settled like a sfumato, a blurring.

The subtlety of birds. They all look the same, it's almost impossible to truly see them. You can hear them, but how are you supposed to identify which one is singing when? How to connect sound to sight? Birds are fleeting, mobile. It's hard to know where they are. At times they're nothing more than a soundtrack, and you no longer pay them any mind: animals turned white noise.

Then suddenly they become ghostly voices, trills without bodies, mysteries amid the dreams of a siesta.

On the very green grass, the dry shed skin of a snake.

I'm a man soaking up the sun without a shirt on. Lying on thin canvas in the grass. March sun, siesta sun. Humidity rises from the ground. A plane goes by.

The plants are thriving in the garden. Everything is growing, greening, the sun still warms but no longer burns.

Just a little bit of wind. A world of very quiet things. Immobile things. A vase filled with zinnias. A hummingbird comes to visit the sage. The black acacias are already wearing their pods: tight on the branches, they hang a little lax, a little ridiculous. They haven't darkened yet, they're tender, newly donned, apple green, bright, almost phosphorescent. The chinaberry, too, heavy with new little drupes. One by one the leaves of the mulberry tree fall.

The grass scattered with the dry leaves of the eucalyptus tree.

Wind in the highest part of the treetops. Below, quiet. You can feel it above, at the tip of the branches, but below nothing moves. Only the leaves of the phoenix palm from time to time, brushing the sheet metal of the ceiling of the little room. And the rumination of the cows, nearby, in the pasture. Hearing them ripping out the grass by rolling it around the tips of their tongues. They roll up a section of grass, pull, and chew, slowly. A couple of annoying flies.

Moths in the verbenas.
Dust that has settled on the leaves.
Bird tracks in the guadal of the road.

There's nothing more delightful than long emails with lots of sections, emails that don't seem like free emails so much as letters sent by airmail, squeezing as much information as possible into the same dispatch, communication spaced out in time, spaced out simply because the letter must cross space.

I'd like to be able to describe Zapiola better. The house. The land around it. The road behind it. I'd like to talk all about it with someone who lives far away, in another province, another landscape, another country. A very long email, and I'd like for whoever receives it to be able to see, as they read, Zapiola as it really is, as if they were here, as if the words were Zapiola, as if the words were all of this.

But on the page, a landscape isn't landscape, but rather the texture of the words you've put it into, the universe those words create.

The experience of a landscape has nothing to do with language. I don't have to figure out how to describe a landscape unless I want to talk about it with someone who isn't familiar with it, and in general, I'd probably prefer to give just a couple of details, because I know that in the end, the exercise is necessarily in vain.

I experience the landscape by way of my eyes, my skin, my ears, but I can't put it into words. I don't even try to. Or I try to only here, for myself, a few key words in order not to forget. Door words that in ten, fifteen years, after some time has passed, will open me to the memory of my body moving through these places, to the sensations and feelings of this time in my life.

First there is an intimate, reckless naming, baptisms as boundary markers to compartmentalize the landscape and to tame it: Abandoned House Road, Forest Rectangle Road, the little hill with the poplars. Ways to colonize the pampas with labels.

Only when others come into the picture do we start to put words to things for real. To separate the landscape into parts. To pay attention to what is the most notable, what two or three key elements must be mentioned in order for the other person to be able to reconstruct the whole: to categorize, prioritize, select. All ways of describing, of verbalizing on behalf of someone else, so that they, in some way, even if it's vicarious, can be a part of your experience.

Replicating an experience in language, despite the fact that language cannot transmit the experience.

As though reading the description of taking a walk in the countryside could be the same as taking a walk in the countryside.

Virginia Woolf, trying to reproduce in her sentences the rhythms of her walks. Adjectives like curves, adverbs like slopes, subordinate clauses like little detours, assonances and cacophonies like refuse by the side of the road.

Mysteriously, the narration of landscape that at first seems doomed to failure ends up actually enhancing the landscape for me. Trying to put it into words forces me to look at it in detail and in depth.

Sometimes, there are things that, unless we possess a name for them, do not exist: a particular cloud, a particular tree, a particular weed.

Naming the parts of a landscape also gives a true/false sense of ownership.

Crescent moon. A mere paring in the western sky. A dog barks outside. At five the roosters start to crow.

It's cool and, although it's only mid-March, the days break as though it's fully fall now. The grass shimmers with dew. Throughout the night, the house held onto the warmth of afternoon, and in the morning, the windows have all fogged up on the inside.

Ash trees yellowing. First the leaves turn apple green. Then they grow completely yellow. Yellow orbs. They're among the most beautiful things about autumn.

The acacias, too, starting to veer into brown.

Lots of flowering pampas grass. Their white plumes wilt in the distance.

The vegetation of the road covered in dry leaves. The poplar curtain at the entrance begins to thin a little. They almost don't offer shade anymore. Unimpeded sun swings through their branches.

'That natural sadness that the end of summer brings,' Félix Bruzzone says somewhere.

Even though this January vegetable garden was mostly an experiment, a way to get myself excited about something and a way to pass the time, it's definitely taught me that a person has to abide by the seasons. There's no sense in trying to impose any particular rhythm on nature, because nature already has its own rhythm.

I've also learned that the soil here is hard and clayey, and in order to make things a little easier, you have to add a lot of compost to it, organic matter and sand. I've learned that potatoes don't do well in this region, that everything needs to be sown when it needs to be sown, that everything needs to be protected from the birds, that you can try broken rice on the ants but that the only thing that really works is liquid ant killer, that pumpkins shouldn't be planted in holes, but rather close to the surface, and that then you have to earth up the stems to keep them above ground so that when you water them, they won't stagnate.

The radishes turned out badly again. More things I've learned: radishes must be planted in rows, in full sun, when the moon is waning, and they have to be thinned as soon as possible.

And the arugula is going to seed.

With so much humidity, the dry leaves of the poplar trees begin to rot on the ground and, after being dotted with grey specks, they become dark brown, almost black.

The yellow leaves of the acacia fall on the bright green grass. They are metal sheets, like coins that float, dragged along a little by the wind.

The eucalyptus leaves turn around and around as they fall, slowly, but straight down.

The chicks grow, and now they are poised about halfway between chickhood and henhood. Teenagers. They already have their red feathers, but underneath, in patches, in certain spots, you can still make out that soft yellow down. Little by little they've been shedding it. For now, they are skinny, mangy birds, a little stunted-looking, a little lanky. Awkward and easily scared.

Almost nine, and the sun won't come up. Intense fog. Surrounded by fog. Covered in fog. Shrouded in fog. Living in fog.

The cows don't seem to realize. You can't see them, can only barely hear their quiet grazing out in the field.

The eucalyptus trees drip. The dew accumulates on their leaves, slides down, falls in irregular drops: one here, one there, in a haphazard rhythm, or in no rhythm.

The drops resound on the drowned tin roof, grey of darkened zinc.

The doves' flight is quiet. You can only guess they're there by the faint buzz of wings in the white, milky air.

Some birds can hardly be heard at all.

No parrots yet. Parrots are creatures of the sun.

All the pages of the book I'm reading ripple. The corners fold up.

It's not cold.

The spider webs on the araucaria are covered in dewdrops.

APRIL

Siesta. The smell of Raid in the kitchen and the intermittent buzzing of the flies that are slowly dying, their
little legs up in the air, on the window lintel, on the
tablecloth, on the tiles and the granite countertop.

I close my eyes, stay in bed for a while but can't quiet
my thoughts. As tired as I am, I can't get to sleep.

I get up, open my computer, click on the icon to
create a new file. The cursor flashes, lonesome in the upper
left-hand corner, while the rest of the page is a translucent,
electric white. Outside, not a hint of wind. Inside the only
thing that can be heard is the death throes of the flies. It's a
temperate afternoon, with dazzling sun. Suddenly: a noise
in the backyard. A great crack and a loud thud that echoes
through the earth. I go outside to see what's going on. Out
of nowhere, an enormous eucalyptus branch has collapsed,
taking with it branches of the ash tree and missing the
wire fence of the sheep pen by only half a metre.

I weed the plot by the drive and sow more arugula,
pincushion flowers, a bit of mustard, cilantro, parsley.
I transplant some small leeks, some onions that have
sprouted in the basket in the kitchen.

Luiso comes and stares at the fallen branch.

That's how eucalyptus is, it'll never warn you, he says. It'll stay where it is in a storm and then, out of the blue, it'll go from being sound as a bell to collapsing. Same thing happened to a woman in town: she went down to open her gate, and a eucalyptus branch hanging right over her head just up and fell.

Did it kill her?

Luiso shakes his head.

Missed her by ten centimetres, he says. That's fate for you: when it's your turn, it's your turn. And when it ain't, it ain't.

So then what happened?

Nothing. Nothing happened after that, Luiso says. After that the gal had all her eucalyptus trees chopped down.

Luiso goes to inspect the fence while I begin sowing a second batch of cabbage, broccoli, and various types of kale in a couple of plug trays and put in three trays of new lettuce where I'd previously had the watercress that never came up.

As I sow, I think that if the woman had been crushed by the eucalyptus branch, it would have been a story (the start of a story, or the end of a story, or the climax in the third act of a story), but since the branch didn't crush her, it's only an anecdote: it's not enough to be a story.

In the middle of my grandfather's wake, my brother whispered in my ear: get Juanca to tell you about Demarchi's big trip.

What happened to Demarchi? I asked my cousin.

He motioned for me to follow him into the kitchen, away from the clusters of old men conversing in hushed voices and the circle of women reciting the rosary.

Demarchi had a sister who had got cancer and died, my cousin told me. Demarchi's daughters were too young to understand what had happened, but they were very sad, so one day Demarchi sat them down and told them not to worry, that their aunt had gone to heaven and that she was looking down on them, and looking out for them, from there.

Demarchi suffered greatly from the death of his sister. He was in a bad, a very bad way, he needed a change, there were days when he couldn't even get out of bed, so he decided to take a road trip up north with his two girls and his wife in his F100.

The F100 is a real glutton, it uses a ton of fuel, said my cousin, so Demarchi drove slow. They stopped along the way: Tucumán, Salta, some landscapes, all very gorgeous. Then they made it to Jujuy, and Demarchi said to his wife that since they'd already made the long trip there, they might as well take the Train to the Clouds. Demarchi asked about it at a tourist office: each ticket cost a lot of money, and there were four of them. Why spend a fortune if there was also a road, and the F100 would have no issues making the climb?

It would take a full day to do it, but who cared? They had time. So they went out early, ready to head up the mountain, as high as the train. They went up and up and up. They went so high up that at some point they started getting altitude sickness. Demarchi felt as if he had an elephant's foot pressing down on his chest, he thought he was going to have a heart attack, thought he was going to die. His wife's nose began to bleed. The girls' ears were hurting.

It'll pass, it'll pass, don't worry, Demarchi said to them as they kept going up, until finally they reached a realm where mountains were embedded in clouds, and the clouds enveloped them, and they were surrounded by clouds and wet air and a grey mist that they could feel with their fingers, just by reaching their hands out the windows, and that from time to time opened up and from time to time thickened and closed in again.

What is this? asked one of the girls.

These are the clouds, Demarchi said.

And then:

Are we going to heaven to visit our aunt? asked his other daughter excitedly, just as a little blood began to pool in both her ears.

Then, in the middle of the wake, I burst out laughing. It was the anecdote of the afternoon. We dragged anyone who came in over to my cousin so he could tell them what had happened to Demarchi.

And after the funeral, when we went home, all of us tired, all of us sad, and someone opened up the fridge, and we got to snacking on cheese and olives and leftovers from the day before, painstakingly recapping the wake, who had been there, who hadn't been able to make it, who'd sent their condolences, who looked old, who we couldn't even recognize, again and again that anecdote about Demarchi came up in our conversation.

The time Demarchi got on the Train to the Clouds in his F100, and the girls thought they were going to heaven to visit their dead aunt.

A way to communicate with one another, to say what we weren't brave enough to say.

We're grownups. We'd be embarrassed to comfort one another with the idea that our grandfather had gone to heaven, and so we told the story of Demarchi: a kind of companionship, a form of consoling, of alleviating the pain and the grief.

We communicate with one other in stories, in anecdotes, in fictions.

A form of not communicating.

A kind of companionship.

Foggy sunrise. The goldenness of the sun fades into the air. The dew reveals a spiderweb between the thistles, smaller webs over the grass.

A day of lounging around and doing nothing and of getting a little bit bored. I decide to try my luck with one of the unfinished short stories, again. I sit and work at it for a while, but then I give up. I can't figure out the tone, I can't figure out the narrator. Seen from the first sentence, the story gives the impression of a very high hill, something I won't even be able to start climbing, let alone reach the top of. I used to be able to, but not anymore. Something broke, I'm not ready yet. I'm not ready.

I take the deck chair out by the chicken coop, release the chickens and sit watching them. They are chickens who never saw their mother, who were born in an incubator and yet, without having anyone to model themselves on, they act like chickens: their movements, their habits, their way of scrabbling at the ground, lifting their heads, taking fright at every little thing that happens. They're funny, and they're quite stupid.

After digging through the dry leaves for a while, one of them finds a big beetle, lifts it, clenching it in her beak, and runs away. She doesn't want to share it with the others, but nor is she able to eat it. When she has attained a certain distance, a certain guarantee of solitude, she drops the beetle and pecks at its shell, once, twice, three times, as if trying to crack it. She watches it, pecks at it again in vain. In the end she swallows it whole, and you can almost see the bulge of the beetle descending her neck, the live beetle kicking in her crop and roving and moving around. The hen clears her throat at some length, then carries on as though nothing had happened, scrabbling around in the grass and taking pecks at everything she crosses paths with.

Today I harvested the first batch of spinach. The lettuce I sowed in the furrow got out of control, I never thinned them out, and it rained too much. They were tumultuous, and they were about to go bad. I cut a lot of it. The Chinese cherry tomato plant keeps on producing.
Lots of arugula, lots of lettuce, lots of tomatoes.
The zinnias are still in bloom.

As I have dinner, an icy wind picks up, almost out of nowhere, and it gets cooler. The wind blows all night.
There's nothing more disturbing than wind at night.
It continues blowing in the morning.
It reminds me of Cabrera, where one day you'll get a north wind, and the next a south one. But it is always windy, ceaselessly windy, windy all the time.

Windy days exhaust me, demoralize me, make me think neurotically, put me in a foul mood.
I need for something to keep still, at least for a little while.

I buy some food in Lobos for the wild cat that lives in the woodpile and leave it on a plate by the kitchen door. As I'm reading out on the veranda, I hear him eating. That discreet gnashing of his teeth crushing the pellets of dry food. I peek around the corner, and the cat runs off.

Missh, mish, mish, I call, and the cat stops in the distance, near where the orange tree is, and stares at me. I prepare a saucer of milk for him, set it out, go back to reading. I peek around the corner again, again he runs off. I call him, he stops, he stares. The scene repeats three or four times. He's hungry, but he's not yet confident enough to come and eat in my presence.

I let the hens out to graze a while outside the chicken coop. They dig among the fallen leaves of the eucalyptus trees, they dig in the damp earth under the hydrangeas, they dig in the dry grass. They draw their legs back and incline their heads forward, lowering them so they are almost level with the ground. If there is a noise, they swivel their heads up, alert.

When I turn to them again, they've got into my vegetable garden and are digging in the thyme and oregano. I shoo them away, but they're insistent. They are docile chickens: when I get close, they immediately flatten themselves against the ground, as though I were a rooster looking to mount them. I pick them up, carrying one under each arm. They ride very still and calm, with their heads held high, gazing out at everything from this new height. As I walk to the coop, I pet their crops with my hand. Beneath their soft feathers, the crop is a ball, a bit smaller than a tennis ball. On my fingertips I can feel the texture of cracked corn, of bugs and gravel, of all their morning food.

That's enough for today, you've eaten plenty, I tell them as I close them in.

'Every family has its own collection of stories, but not every family has someone to tell them,' says Lyn Hejinian. I have my grandmother.

Sometimes, in winter, when there was nothing left to do, and outside the afternoon was grey, leaden, and an icy cold had descended over the landscape, in the little house, lit up in the wind, my grandmother would take her box of photographs down from the highest shelf of the closet. It was a cardboard box, almost a cube, that someone, possibly my mother, had long ago lined with a cloth covered in tiny blue flowers. Inside, loose, there were hundreds of old photos. Small photos, 5 x 9 cm, with a white border that framed them, scalloped, most of them slightly arching upwards, warped. Postcard-sized photos, some pasted to a harder backing, others loose, almost always newly baptized babies. Photos with worn-away edges, with fungal spots burbling up in big blobs or like sepia-coloured welts dotted across the image's yellowish surface. Larger photos, generally inside a kind of posterboard folder with a lid and covered with a sheet of tracing paper, or parchment paper so brittle and dry you'd be right to be frightened to touch it. These, in general, were photos of newlyweds (in the oldest pictures, the brides didn't even wear white, but rather a sober black) or of silver anniversaries, golden anniversaries. Couples, the man always seated, the woman standing, a little bit behind, her hands resting on the back of the chair, slowly growing old. Photos that had crossed the ocean, the only memory of parents left behind in Italian graves, of dead siblings, siblings impossible to locate.

Grandma would sit at the head of the table, put on her glasses, take out a picture at random, look at it – only barely raising her nose to access the lower part of her bifocals – and tell me who they were.

This is Uncle Bauta the day he came back from his military service, she said and handed me the picture.

These were some friends of Nòno's who came to see

us one day. I don't recall what their names were. They were from Cañada de Gómez.

Here we were during the Slaughter Days on Aunt Anita's farm. The one on the end is your grandfather, next to him is Uncle Mingo, Uncle Pirín, that one down there is our poor late Ángel Alberto, and this one is Uncle Francisco.

What about that one? I asked, pointing out a smiling man at the edge of the table who was holding up an empty bottle as if it were a sword or a trophy.

Grandma took the photo back, extending her arm, moving the image closer and then farther away. She raised and lowered her head to view it through the bottom and the top parts of her glasses.

I don't recall that one, she said. Must have been one of the guys who worked with Aunt Anita.

Out of the photos in the box, I had my favourites. As Grandma talked and told me stories of all those strangers who made up our family, I would sort through the stacks, my nimble fingers flicking past photo after photo until I'd come across the ones I liked the most.

This is from Mario's baptism, and these here are from my wedding day, Grandma said.

These are the photos from when Nòna turned eighty: we celebrated in the big shed, which had just been built, look how new the walls were. Your grandfather had finished painting it that week, to get it ready for the party.

Easy, easy, be careful, my grandma said as I rummaged around for more pictures.

What about these guys? I asked and showed her a photo of five men dressed in black double-breasted suits and hats, in very serious poses, alongside a stream, with shotguns and pistols in their hands, a tuff ravine and dry weeds behind them, a mix of gangsters and Wild West.

Grandma took the photo and looked at it for a split second, then smiled.

Those are the Giraudo uncles.

How come they have revolvers? I asked, despite knowing the answer.

I think the shotguns were real, my grandma always said, but the revolvers were probably just toys.

Where were they going? To a party?

No, no, no, my grandmother said, shaking her head.

It was the day the photographer came, they dressed up as outlaws.

Why'd they dress up?

Grandma shrugged.

That's just how they were, she said. They were funny, they were pranksters.

And this one? I asked and handed her another photo.

This was a day we had finished the threshing. At that time, you'd gather the corn into heaps and then the threshing machine would come. That's me there, the littlest one. The one farthest back is Aunt Teresa, and the one holding on to the wheel is Uncle Tonito.

Outside, the scant light of the afternoon sun would be slowly going out. Grandma would go to the garden to pull some carrots and gather a little chard. She would wash them in the basin, under a powerful stream of cold water. I'd remain seated at the head of the table, taking the black-and-white photos one by one and, although I already knew all of them by heart, I would examine them again in silence, for a long while, taking my time.

There was something about those old photographs that dazzled me, as though instead of originating in some long-ago time, they came from a far-off space: a different land, another world, another universe. A place where six black horses pulled the carriages for burials, where a town square was a fenced-off box with no trees in the middle of nowhere, and the church just a solitary structure rising out of grass that was sparse, cut short, still.

One by one I went through and separated the photos into different categories, according to who was in them, or what branch of the family. And then, within those categories, I'd select someone, some character, and I'd make little piles of their pictures. Uncle Bautista's pile, Aunt Catalina's pile, a pile for one of the Uncles Giraudo, although it was hard for me to tell them apart, and I always ended up mixing them up. I'd keep the rest of the photos in the box and, on the smooth white vinyl surface of the table, I'd organize with perfect care the pictures of a given character, one after the next, in chronological order, like dominoes: baptisms striking first communions, first communions hitting fifteenth birthdays, or pictures in military uniforms, soldiers' uniforms, grenadiers'. Young guys, bachelors out on the town, along with wedding photos, some honeymoon photos, almost always the couple perched on a rock in the mountains and then, soon after, pictures of growing families: first just a baby in the wife's lap, then a child in a pushchair and another baby in her lap. Always a baby in her lap, as taller and taller boys and girls joined in around them, in suits and shorts, with black ribbons in their hair, girls in dresses covered in bows, young men with moustaches and hats.

As my grandmother prepared our meal, and the steam from the pots billowed against the kitchen window, I would go over, very slowly, as though I were studying an extremely complex text, one after another of that progression of images that made up a life. I'd stare into every detail, every smile, every hat; I'd look, and I would memorize Uncle Bauta's life, and the life of Aunt Teresa, my grandfather's life, Uncle Tonito's. The shoes, the backgrounds painted with landscapes of palm trees from the wedding photos; the arms that rested on the shoulder of a friend; the slight consternation of a woman tying back her apron as she is photographed among the chickens; a baby lying on its own, face down on a table; the signatures, the stamps of the photographers: Casa Bedolla, in golden strokes of calligraphy that do a thousand somersaults and wrap up in a wild flourish; the spot, right by the corner, where a triangle in the carpet had been folded over, revealing the dirt floor of the makeshift studio in the middle of the plains.

Until Grandma would say:
All right, that's enough for now, let's put them away. Go call Uncle Tonito, go call Grandpa. Dinner's ready.

I'm still harvesting tomatoes. One zucchini survives. One zapallito. Two cucumbers.

The lettuce sprouted nicely. The mustard. The chard. The cilantro and parsley came up looking good. Dry poplar leaves mixed in with my crops. Under where one leaf fell, the seeds have become just pale skinny shoots, long and twisting. One by one I collect the dry leaves and take them to the compost bin, so that these shoots will straighten out and grow.

The black ants have eaten all of the cotyledons off of the marigolds, it would be hard for them to bounce back. The Red Russian kale looks great, but the cauliflower barely even sprouted.

The nights are cool now. The countryside here isn't like it is in Córdoba. Here autumn doesn't mean drought and dull colours. Here autumn is dew and humidity. Foggy in the morning. Everything turns green.

A clear and diaphanous night, crystalline. Lots of stars. Crescent moon. Moon among the acacias. Silvery or bluish moonlight.

The last remnants of summer languish. The zinnias get scraggly. The marigolds dry up. The green beans are on their way out. The squash plants, already weakened with age, are covered with powdery mildew, same as the cucumber plants. I pull them out whole. I amputate stems, roots. Toss them out with no compunction. Make room for the new. Back and forth and back and forth to the composting bin. I only leave the zinnias, the stronger ones, since they're still blooming. Trying to follow the cycle.

It is the season for cutting firewood for the winter and storing it up indoors, so that it can finish drying, so that the rain and the dew don't get into it. It's cool, and there is sunshine, but large clouds float across the sky, and at times, they cover the sun completely. An autumn day. Last night it rained a lot, so everything in the garden was damp and drooping.

The wild cat turned out to be a female. Yesterday two kittens were meowing around in the wood. Then one, completely black, flashed by on its way to the eucalyptus. I tried to catch it, but I couldn't, it was fast, and it was not friendly. It slipped right out of my hands. They're not that little. I looked for them all afternoon, but I didn't see them again.

I ask Luiso.

They rarely get the chance to grow up, he says. The chimangos will get to kittens about as soon as they're born out here. The second they let their guard down, they pluck them up and carry them off in the air.

A kitten walking through the grass, the shadow of a bird of prey passing over it, claws digging into the back of its neck, a kitten taking flight.

If it were fiction, it would be the start of a beautiful adventure: a litter of kittens, on an expedition to the swamp, with the aim of rescuing their sibling from its kidnapping.

Or a kitten that escapes the evil chimango, the adventure of going home, overcoming a million obstacles and making friends along the way.

One of the few things Luiso genuinely hates is his neighbour. Whenever he gets the chance, he speaks ill of him. He complains about the smell of the pigs, he complains about the noise made by the machine that grinds the corn, he complains about the flies, he says that everything over there is filthy, that the guy does nothing but accumulate mice, that his dogs killed one of the sheep, that he doesn't feed them anything and then they come and bother the calves.

I always sense, between the lines, other reasons, older fights, slights, offenses I intuit but that Luiso doesn't quite say, at least not in so many words.

That pig smell is about to come to an end, he said yesterday before he left, tilting his head in that neighbour's direction.

Why? Is he selling the pigs?

It can't be long before he goes under, he said. People in town have been talking. Talking about how he won't pay his workers, how he doesn't treat his workers well, how they're all going to walk out on him.

I nodded. I didn't say anything.

It's not the first time it's happened to him, Luiso continued. His cheese factory that he inherited from his dad went bust. At some point he had chickens, but that's over, too. After that he started buying grains, he'd buy them and sell them on the black market, pay for them in instalments over sixty days, ninety days. Until one time around we just didn't see him again, he disappeared with the cash and filed for bankruptcy. He took a lot of guys to the cleaners, but just try and get him to pay anybody what he owes. He's a bad man. That's why he doesn't live here anymore, he moved down to Lobos, and he drives back and forth every day.

I thought he lived here, I said.

No, no, he lives in Lobos. You never noticed that every time he gets in his truck he heads in that direction? How could he live here when everyone in town hates his guts? It's a shame because he's got little kids. Now he has this thing with the pigs, but that's not going to last, either, because he's already screwed it all up again. I know what I'm talking about. I know him, he's married to my sister.

I didn't know he was your brother-in-law, Luiso. What does your sister have to say about it?

Luiso shrugged.

Well, what do you expect her to say? She works like a mule, claims he's just got bad luck.

Very early this morning, screams woke me up. It was barely light outside, and it was cold. Frightened, I quickly got dressed and went out to see what was going on. That same neighbour had left his truck parked in front of our gate with the engine on. He was cursing. He was tearing up clumps of grass and flinging them into the air, kicking his fender and pounding on the hood of his truck with his fist clenched.

Fuck you, Christ, he was shouting, fuck you, Mother of God. What the fuck did I do? What is it you're trying to tell me I've done wrong? He was alone. The dogs were circling around him, tussling.

Of course I'd come down with fucking cancer! Of course I'd get fucking cancer and fucking everything would go to shit! our neighbour screamed.

Fucking piece of fucking shit! Goddammit mother-fucker fuck! he said.

One of the dogs responded to his shouting with a howl, another went to piss on his truck.

Get out! Get out of here! The neighbour threw a stick at them. Get out of here, you fucking dogs!

Christ almighty and the fucking cunt of the fucking Virgin, he said.

Sunny morning, a cold wind that stings your face. Cloudless sky. Cold. The wind rustles in the few leaves that remain on the poplar by the driveway. When they no longer have any leaves left, the poplars will be silent.

I set up two smaller beds against the fence. I sow more chard and more calendulas. Pincushion flowers. Delphinium. Sweet peas and more pincushion flowers next to the compost bin.

The autumn flies are heavy, slow. Half dazed by the cold, annoying.

Lots of horseflies in the afternoon. Their bites sting.

There are still mosquitoes.

This is the season when the ants eat everything, starting to store up for winter.

One of the best things about this summer was the zinnias. The marigolds and the nasturtiums. Flowers I will definitely sow again when winter's over.

The fragrance that rises from the leaves of the carrots when you move them aside, looking for which to pull first.

An islet of flowering carquejas next to the road.

In the countryside, and more so in autumn and winter, a house is a refuge. You can feel, in your body, the immensity that surrounds it. A house in the country takes the form of a great silence. Its interior is warmth. Tungsten light. Smell of toast and coffee with milk.

There were almost no books in my grandparents' house in the country. A copy of the Bible, sure, a couple of catechisms, a book by Mariano Grondona, another called *That's How Argentines Do Things*, by an author whose name I don't remember. And stacked on a shelf in the closet in my room, amid folded sheets and towels, packs of candles and brochures from recent ag expos at the Rural Society of Río Cuarto, a few old books from the first Biblioteca Billiken collection, from when my mother was a child. Abridged versions of *The Prince and the Pauper* and *Oliver Twist*. A sort of biography of San Martín called *The Liberator's Sabre*, and another of his daughter Merceditas.

I'd read and reread them.

In stretches of boredom, in the long siestas of broiling summers, in the long nights of icy winters.

There were, too, the *Selecciones by Reader's Digest*. My grandfather subscribed, and they came like clockwork every month, the newspaperman would hand them to him along with a magazine called *Small Farm* and the paper, *The Voice of the Interior* on weekdays and, on Sundays, *The Nation*.

Selected *Selecciones*: 'Laughter, the Best Medicine,' 'All in a Day's Work.' A plot summary of this or that book: it was always some mountaineer with his foot trapped between boulders, or a family locked in a car, at the mercy of murderous bears digging their claws into the hood, piercing the metal, or dread-inducing motorcycle gangs, in the night, chasing a woman crossing the desert alone, all the windows of her car closed and her air conditioning broken.

I think it was there, in an article in *Selecciones*, where I read for the first time that *biography* means *the line of a life*.

Bio-graphy: the drawing, the shape made by the line of a life as it extends across the page/over time.

A lifetime like a drawing that gradually, day after day, forms on a blank page.

And the responsibility of that line to produce something: a harmonious, a clear, an intelligible shape. Its responsibility to produce a drawing.

Anxiety and responsibility in the face of every decision. Every decision an angle that sets the course of a contour in the picture to be drawn by our lives.

And now, as I break up topsoil and transplant onions, I start to see that I don't really like the picture my life has been drawing, or that it's different from what I'd imagined, or maybe: that it's impossible to make any sense of?

A drawing covered in scratches, corrections, false steps, plans falling apart, projects failing, loved ones who stop loving back, who say that's it, get out, get out of here.

Morning of isolated showers. Big high fluffy clouds in the sky. Suddenly they're everywhere, altering the light. Now the sky is completely cloudy. In Spanish, *encapotado*: such a beautiful word. Layered over: overcast. Grey clouds, low, very close together. From time to time their edges can be gleaned, and behind them, higher up, you can see patches of the clearest, bluest sky.

As if out of nowhere, the wind rises, a lash, a bolt of thunder, a flash. The sky gets dark. The downpour lasts five minutes. Then the sun comes out and shines, although it's only barely warming.

The plants droop after the rain. Patches of defeated grasses, weighed down by the water.

All gleaming. The colours shine against the leaden blue of the storm moving on into the distance.

Wet dog smell. Smell of enclosure, of damp inside the closet, inside the house.

I go out into my garden a while, take the opportunity to transplant all the cabbages from the first crop. The rest is weeding. Continuing to take out the dead and dying plants. Loosening the soil to create another bed.

Some of the pigeons coo three notes. Others five.

I'd like to know more about birds. There was a time when trees were to me as birds are now: trees, just a bunch of trees, a shapeless mass of trees. I paid scant attention to them and could recognize only a few, the easiest ones, the most common: Chinaberry, plane, ash – because there were ash trees on the streets of Cabrera. When I started studying botany and taxonomic tables, little by little I began to recognize and distinguish them better. Each one had a name, each traits of its own, a species. And in this way, my world began expanding.

I'd like to be able to pay the same attention to birds

and have them not just be 'birds'. But they're too fast, too often in motion, or too far away.

At the moment, I only recognize the crested caracara, the chimangos, the sparrows, the mockingbirds (although I suspect there's more than one type), the guira cuckoo (which we called magpies where I grew up), the cardinals (I've only seen one of those so far), the thrushes, owls, ringdoves and common pigeons, the fork-tailed flycatchers, the great kiskadees (also known as 'uglybugs') and the woodpeckers.

And the parrots, of course.

And the owls.

And the southern lapwings.

Sautéed rice with carrots, tomatoes, peppers, the last squash. Aside from the rice, all of it grew in my garden.

I'm so intrigued by that place I call the forest rectangle. Every time I go into town I pause to look at it a while. In the middle of the undifferentiated plains, a cramped box of trees, like a block, orthogonal, sitting on a flat field. A curtain of black poplars, spiky, severe, makes its edges abundantly clear, more like walls. And inside, behind the walls of leaves, more trees, only trees, so thick and dense it is impossible for the eyes to penetrate. It has a gate, on the side facing in the direction of the town, but I've never noticed any movements around there, nor tyre tracks, and the road that comes out on the other side is covered in tall weeds as though no one has ever travelled it, as though the place might be abandoned.

I'm also intrigued because it's beautiful. You can see it from far away, from the grassed-over road: the late afternoon sun beating down on a perfect block of trees in the middle of nowhere.

These days, moreover, all the poplars are yellow. And inside it seems to have oak trees, or maples. Trees that turn very red, like flames, like fires alive.

On the road, in front of the house, a man on a motorcycle passes by.

A little while later, another man on horseback.

Lots going on in the neighbourhood.

The incessant noise of the neighbour's corn grinder. He has it on for an hour, almost an hour and a half. It's a monotonous, strident bellowing that echoes through the fields, expanding. Then, suddenly, just when the noise has become unbearable, it stops. Sunset. The neighbour has turned off his grinder. The silence is an ever-denser silence, with many layers, mixed with the distant noise of the occasional car, the song of the birds, the creaking of the branches, the wind in the leaves. Little by little, things blue and blur. The trees in the distance are purple masses, their edges untidy, lumpy, frayed. It is almost completely dark now. In the distance you can see the lights of Cañuelas, of Lobos, a slight phosphorescence, illuminating the clouds and forming a pink or faded orange dome. Still in the hammock, I hear noises behind me. Creaks. Footsteps in the dry grass. I get up just in time to see one of the hares hopping past me, serenely, moving in the direction of the field up ahead.

Then the moon comes out. Full, gigantic, very orange, commanding, barely veiled at all by the layer of clouds that becomes, when confronted by its light, thin as mist.

MAY

A chilly day. Wind since dawn. At night the house actually got cold. I slept in a sweatshirt, with the electric stove turned on.

Big chard, ready to thin, the plants that have survived the ants. A second batch of cabbage, kale, and broccoli, late, but growing at a fairly good clip. Some with a third leaf already. Uneven germinations. The Red Express cabbage takes three times as long as the others to emerge. I had already given up on it by the time it finally started to appear.

Dry eucalyptus and magnolia leaves on the exceedingly green grass.

Magnolia leaves, hard and gleaming, yellow, brown.

Long sections of dry eucalyptus bark lying in the grass. Trees that moult, that grow at a cost of slowly, imperceptibly exploding. Like lemmings, throwing their own hides off the cliff.

The grape ivy has almost no leaves left. The few that remain are a coppery, fiery red. Their bare stems like a wave of crisscrossing arteries and veins on the wall of the little shed. Clusters of grapes, scraggly, sparse, black as raisins, but the size of evergreen berries. A thrush and a dove come every afternoon and peck at the ivy grape by grape. There is also a little bird that's always hopping around in the firewood, one of the many whose names I don't know.

That lethargy that comes with the first cold weather. When we don't know if it's that our bodies haven't got used to the new temperatures or if it's the start of a flu. Sloth. Eyes that feel like they're on fire. The feeling that I'd like to stay in bed until it's dark again.

Now, with the cold, the world seems stagnant. The days are short. It's dark by six. In the garden, everything grows slowly. The first chard from thinning. I wash it under running water, sauté it briskly, with a little garlic, in olive oil. That taste that chard always leaves in your mouth, like powdered iron, rough on the surface of your teeth.

Suddenly it feels like I've been wearing long sleeves, sweaters, fleeces for years, years of not feeling the sun on my skin, even though my shorts are still there on the chair, from the last time I wore them, three weeks ago. Winter slows everything down.

I wake up at four in the morning. A large waning moon rises over the horizon. Just a faded orange fingernail in the black sky. Orange like the orange of tungsten lights.

At dawn, the sun comes on.
Red, mobile, but silent.

Motions in the void. My regular routes, paths stamped into the grass now from so much toing and froing in the garden, feeding the chickens. I read that, according to Corita Kent, one purpose of art is to call our attention to things we might otherwise miss. Those paths, that motion through, actions on air, every day. Those traces. Those tracks.

The first Juan, my grandfather's father, arrived in Argentina in 1915 or 1917. He came from Italy, from the Piedmont region, near the Alps. He was a peasant, the son of peasants, the grandchild of peasants. His family – our family – lived in a small village at the foot of the mountains, tending livestock, growing grapes. They had never been to Rome, or Turin. Only once or twice had they travelled, on foot, down to Cuneo.

The first Juan didn't speak a word of Spanish, nor even Italian. He spoke only a dark, closed Piedmontese. When he disembarked his ship in Buenos Aires, he was just a teenager. His parents were already dead. An uncle who was a priest had made him take the trip: he read the newspaper, and he knew people, and he knew that war was imminent and that if Juan stayed in Italy, he was going to die.

The first Juan didn't know anyone in Argentina, he didn't know what to do, he had nowhere to go. He sat down on some canvas-wrapped bundles and waited. Time passed. People hurried past him. Commotion of cities. Commotion of ports. Night was creeping up, and the first Juan began to cry. Another Italian, also from Piedmont, came and asked him what was the matter, consoled him, told him he knew where to get food, where to sleep. That night, as they shared a meal, the man urged Juan not to stay in Buenos Aires. What was someone like him going to do in Buenos Aires? People here are crazy, he told him. There are a lot of thieves here, all kinds of crooks. Come with me to Córdoba to work the harvest. They have everything you need up there. Plenty of work, plenty of land.

That's our origin myth. My grandfather – the second Juan – used to tell it all the time. Over and over again he'd repeat the same story: a war that expels, a man who arrives out at elbows, without a peso to his name, a dangerous city, empty plains that offer shelter, a place deep in the pampas, so that his children, so that his grandchildren, so that his great-grandchildren, might found a humble kingdom there.

They travelled by train. From Buenos Aires to Villa María. The landscape, from the window, was completely different from everything the first Juan had known up till now: here there were plains, vast distances, loneness, a far-off and continuous horizon. They changed trains. Not a soul by the tracks. No one between town and town, only clear, vacant, available grassland. There weren't even fences: the pampas were still unpartitioned, undivided then.

The towns were more like hamlets, embankments where the train would pause a little while, a few bare trees, an adobe mercantile, three or four huts, a house or two of brick, and the whole circle of the horizon, distant, immense.

In the promised land there were no mountains to shadow the valley, there were no peaks to climb, there were no far-off places to gaze down at from on high. The plain was an enormous void, and at times, it allowed them to believe that they could fill it. They got off at

Las Perdices. They continued by coach, they continued on foot, they slept out in the open, among the scrub, spotting, here and there, a light that would tremble in the night: an early house, settlers in the countryside.

I travel to Cabrera, to visit my family. The highway runs parallel to the old Route 9, which in turn runs along the train tracks that once took the first Juan to where he'd have us.

I leave Zapiola early. Up to Rosario, I don't get bored: there's quite a bit of traffic, I listen to music, the news, local programmes from Ramallo, from San Nicolás. Then, the highway gets perfectly straight. This goes on for miles and miles. I pass almost no other cars. It's a winter day, but the sun is out. I lose radio signals and cell reception. To either side, soybean fields and eucalyptus groves appear and disappear in rapid succession. The landscape I see is always the same flat line. I drive deeper and deeper into the country, deeper into the plain.

I remember my grandfather always talked about how when he was a boy, before radios existed, they calculated the time of day and set their clocks by adding half an hour to the sunrise written on their tear-off calendars. At the base of each sheet, beneath the big digit of the date, the calendar said what time the sun would rise. If it said 6:20 in Buenos Aires, they'd just add thirty minutes, because it would take the planet thirty minutes to cover the distance between Buenos Aires and that little town lost in the middle of the pampas. So they had to wait, looking out at the horizon, for the exact moment when the first smidgen of an arc would peek over the horizon, to run and fix the hands of the clock in the kitchen. The sun rose, 6:20 a.m. in Buenos Aires plus 30 minutes = 6:50. It is exactly ten to seven on this part of the plain.

Thirty minutes' difference. When it's dawn in Zapiola, in the Province of Buenos Aires, it's still night there.

I'm the one who got far away.

That half hour, between dawn here and dawn there, when distance is darkness.

Noon. The rays of the sun shoot straight down. The highway continues to have very little traffic. Just a few trucks, very occasionally. Driving becomes easy, monotonous. Without a fixed point ahead, with cruise control, your spirits rove, your mind wanders. Not long ago, just a couple of years ago, I made another trip like this, on the day I got word that my grandfather was dying. 'He'll last until he decides to go,' said the voice on the other end of the line. 'It's a question of hours, at the most of days.'

Speeding up to be faster than the sun, speeding up to cut distances, speeding up to say goodbye, not to be far away, speeding up to outpace death.

I cried and drove, sensing more than seeing the straight highway past my tears, under the sun of a September afternoon. I cried, and from time to time I took one hand off the steering wheel to wipe my runny nose with the back of my hand. I was afraid my grandpa would be scared, and I thought that the only thing to do was soothe him, help him face what had to happen, be by his side on that journey. Say to him: It's okay, you're dying. Are you frightened? Do you want to do it here? Would you rather be at home?

I imagined that perhaps he, who was old and wise, might crave a medieval deathbed, might want to decide he would die and call everyone up, one by one, to say goodbye, and then sleep until his spirit unfettered itself and gradually left.

I fantasized that maybe we could take him back out into the country and set him up in the middle of a green field, a field of oats, and let him fall asleep there, peaceful, full, placid. The king of that kingdom, the one who had been born on that land and who had never left, who had made such an effort not to ever have to leave, to take root, to stay, not to be carried away in the wind, not to be swallowed by the void.

Hot tears fogged up the lenses of my glasses. Thinking about his thick, broad, soft hands, hands numbed from so much straining with pliers, with hammers, heavy hands, muscular from working the land. I was thinking about my grandfather pointing out some little birds squatting among the stubble, a fox crossing the road, my grandfather telling me about his land, his story, showing me the fields, smiling at what he had achieved, detailing his plans for the next round of sowing.

The colours of the plains in winter. Grandpa dancing to the rhythm of the harvest music.

A couple of months after his death, I found in a drawer four or five of the little notebooks where he noted down figures, lists of what he needed to do or buy when he went into town. Very small notebooks, to be kept in the front pocket of his shirt, along with a pen, the cap clipped over the fabric's edge. Notebooks that were a blend of agenda and record of yields and rain. I had kept some, just to have them. To see his handwriting again from time to time, neat, even, to be able to reread the casual notes of his days. Little relics/memories I treasure, like the magpie treasures shiny little things in its nest.

Grandfather hunched over the kitchen table, writing slowly, with a black pen, on the tiny pages. On the first page, always, a list of phone numbers.

Titarelli 4050365
Ferrero 4050368
Mario Rosso 155615060
H. Vitali 4050134
Lüining 156003582
Tyre shop 4051600

Weds July 4
Corn Threshing 56720
Stop by the vet's
Farmhand wages, returns. Bonus
Buy buttons/lettuce seeds/chic
Corn threshing 18 ha
Pharmacy, Vic hot tea

Fri July 6
Bank Overview
Peretti Oview
Juanca
Slaught cows. 9 fat
See photocopies invoice
Do not forget: Aldactone. Pharmacy

Fri July 13
Pick up fruit
Dog food. Paint
Ice.
8 am 25-Heifer Truck
Gastaldi
Drill. Find bits

Thurs 19
Las Perdices: 8 Swiss hinges
Disc harrow
Corn 35 ha

Fair cows 7
Dry cows 10
Cows w/o teeth 3
Nursery cows
Brush Rake
Rake. Get garlic

His daily rounds. His motion through, actions on the air of every day.

'How we spend our days is, of course, how we spend our lives,' writes Annie Dillard.

I get off the highway in Villa María. I cross the city, looking for the two-lane road that will take me to the town. By then, I've been behind the wheel for nearly seven hours. An hour left. As always, the trip is long, tiredness weighs on me, little by little the radio stations have returned.

The sun starts to disappear on the horizon. The landscape here is flat and uniform like in Zapiola, but this doesn't look like that. This is good land. This is an agricultural region.

Here there isn't vegetation, only weeds in need of removal.

There are no panicles, or sprigs, there are no natural meadows, no trees that grow on their own, no wild grasses, no swamps or lagoons, there's no chaos, no intermingling, no being left alone. On either side of the road, all is boxed, neat, under control: naked fences, visible to the last wire, grasses kept level with glyphosate, even monoculture, land exploited to the max, soybeans to export to China and collect for in sixty or ninety days.

The beauty of this area – if indeed it has any – is that of the polished, the studiously harmonious, a classic, orderly beauty: right angles, smooth surfaces, flat colours, that which fits into a grid.

Threshing season is coming to an end. Only a few fields left, plants dry and loaded down with seed pods, waiting. Out of the corner of my eye, on the side of the road, rows of harvested stalks and stems. At seventy-five miles per hour, I quickly leave them behind, flickering or vibrating, as if they were a clatter of celluloid, and then they vanish like a fan snapping shut, yellow, beige, light grey.

At the turn for Arroyo Cabral, a large harvester swallows twenty furrows at a time. The sun lights up the cloud of dust that rises in its path, making it sparkle.

I stop to take a piss at the Dalmacio Vélez stream. I turn off the engine. The silence takes me by surprise. All you can hear is the sound of the reeds rubbing up against each other. You can't hear the wind, but it is there, you can see it in the swaying, the slow motions of the reeds, the plumes, the leaves of a green so opaque it almost looks like grey.

The first Juan, my grandfather's father, built his whole life here, on these plains. He got married, had children, planted wheat, planted flax. Day after day, as he shaved in front of the mirror, he saw how the hard water of this area was darkening his teeth. He had the only sister he had left brought over from Italy. He created a family.

Back there, on the other side of the ocean, were the Alps, rocks, hills, the snows in winter, white water when the snow melted, green meadows. There, everything was someone else's, everything was already full: where there were no mountain peaks, there were valleys, slopes in shadow and slopes in full sun, towns, forests, roads. Little plots. There were too many of them, there was not enough space, beds of onions ran up against the train tracks, basil and parsley grew in pots on window-sills. There was no space, there was no place for him, for them.

Over there, there was war. The terror of war coming closer. Dead soldiers.

Here everything is wide open, empty. You have to draw your own boundaries, lest your furrows just go on and on, forever. Here you can see someone coming from a very long way off.

There's space here, you own your land.

You're far away here.

And he was one of the ones who stayed, 'hearing the hearts of the cows', as Alejandro Schmidt writes in a poem.

He died not much past fifty. No one in my family talked a lot about the rest of his life. I assumed they would have been years of routine, of rest, once he had established himself, got a wife, had kids. A rural destiny. The music of the harvests ringing in his ears.

It wasn't until recently that my grandmother let another part of his story slip, a fact that no one until that time had ever stated directly: the first Juan would go out to drink whenever he went into town. He was a depressive, he was an alcoholic, he didn't take care of himself. He finally had a heart attack. It left him paralyzed. After that the family would take him for walks around the vegetable garden, pushing his wheelchair through the clods of earth, showing him the rows of leeks and onions, how full the lemon tree was; placing the first peach, the first plum in his uncooperative hands.

The promised land had turned out to be a rough void, too gruelling to fill.

Planting trees to make shade, to occupy the land, to make firewood, to build fires.

Having kids to work more and more land.

Never a peso to spare.

And on the other side, an origin razed. Burned by war.

Nowhere to go home to.

No Ithaca, not behind him, not ahead of him.

To be trapped in that void.

A life that tries to arise on the plains, and the wind that, over and over, knocks it down.

The last rosary of towns: Dalmacio Vélez, Perdices, Deheza. A girl waiting for the bus at an enclosed stop. Driving behind a truck hauling steers. The smell of fresh dung coming in through the air vents. The looks of the steers between the slats. Quick guinea pigs on the shoulders of the road eating the soybeans that fall out of the trucks. Dry grass that falls like water. A bloated fox, dead by the side of the road.

The dog barks. My mother comes out to greet me. She says she's been anxiously awaiting my arrival, anxiously because I'd come by the highway. She gives me a kiss. It's almost dark out now.

Inside, the stove is on, three or four logs burning. The TV is set to the Rural Channel. Sitting at the table, my father is reading the paper.

Hey, you're here, he says as he looks up.

The freezing fur on the dog's back. His hot breath. His muzzle resting on my leg so I can pet his head, behind his ears.

Papa puts out chorizo, soda, wine. Some bread. Some cheese. He eats standing up, next to the fridge. The dog sits down beside him and looks at him, hoping for a bite of anything.

I cut myself a piece of cheese.

Don't fill up, dinner will be ready in a second, my mother says.

I go out to the patio, find a log, add it to the fire.

All the trees in the municipality painted white up to knee height so that the ants don't climb up the branches, don't climb up the bark. Wreaths of white stones, also painted with lime, very neat, around each new little tree.

Every year the trees get cut back a little more, so that their branches won't come into contact with the power lines. The people who prune them don't care about the trees. They mutilate their crowns, destroy all their inborn harmony. Scars of past pruning on the stumps of the branches stripped now of their leaves.

But continuing to grow, after the cuts and mutilations. Carrying on, growing wherever possible, shapely still, but beautiful no longer.

The trees on either side of the sidewalk can't reach each other. Their branches don't even come close.

Nothing that covers, nothing that provides any shade, any shelter.

It's dark now. The minimal light of the lightbulbs. The orange light coming in from the street. The low houses.

The closed doors. Closed windows, lowered blinds. A glacial cold. No one out. In the distance, on the other side of the town, a truck drives by.

Everyone busies themselves with their own side of the sidewalk, comprehends the world in accordance with the images that filter through the lace curtains at their window.

My father, with his parents, spoke Piedmontese. With us, he spoke Spanish.

When we were kids, on winter afternoons, back before the Rural Channel existed, and it was already dark, and Dad had already read the whole paper and grown bored, he would take from the shelf a large Vox dictionary with a forest green cover, wide as two stacked bricks. He'd set it on the table in front of him and open it at random, start reading about words, one after another, with his reading glasses perched on his nose, his head slightly lowered, the tip of his index finger guiding his eyes down the lines.

He'd read with great concentration, while Mum made dinner and my siblings watched Hola Susana on Telefe, the channel with the logo that was three little coloured balls.

Meanwhile, I would read the magazine that came with the paper on Sundays. Slowly I would turn the pages, looking at the photographs, the bright spaces, the light on objects, the happy people who lived in those far-off places, polished, sharp to perfection, pure.

On the other side of the table, Dad would bring his finger half a centimetre down, read the definition of another word, and look surprised; sometimes it was a surprise like, 'Would you look at that, who would have thought,' and sometimes it was more like confirmation, a 'That's what I figured.' I don't remember him ever making any actual comments about what he was reading. Nor did he systematically add new words to his vocabulary. Although he was obsessed with certain words that he repeated all the time: Honolulu, for example.

I'm going to get you a ticket to Honolulu, he'd always tell my cousin Marisa.

Torombolo was another word he always used, meaning bonbon, or chocolate, or chocolate bonbon.

On winter nights, at the end of dinner, Dad would ask if there were any torombolos.

Then he would send one of us to Pitrola's kiosk, on the corner. Milka. Suchard. Bon o Bon, any brand.

If it was my turn, I'd choose Suchard with raisins, my favourite.

Pitrola hardly ever smiled. He was possessed by bad humour. He was a widower, and he had a severely disabled daughter, Laura, and a son, Mauri, who took almost sole care of his sister. Years later, when Mauri was married and had two children, he got into a car accident as the family was returning from a trip to Río Cuarto. Only his wife survived.

So Don Pitrola tended the kiosk, continued selling chocolates, cigarettes, torombolos, magazines, and the only other people who remained in his household were Laura, strapped to her wheelchair, and Mauri's widow, who spent her days just staring out the window.

Pitrola was unfathomable to us: Why so many trials for just one man? How was he supposed to live?

Now the kiosk is closed, blinds drawn. It looks abandoned.

Was it on those winter nights, buying torombolos from Don Pitrola, that I began to feel I needed to leave Cabrera?

In a small town, each of us is a biography, a row of photos, a continuous thread, our identity affixed to a story, to a history. Three, four, five moments in a person's life that, in some way, make up enough of a sketch to identify us. Misfortunes, accidents, encounters, jobs, loves, births, achievements, funny anecdotes, poignant ones. Milestones on a timeline. Points in a life joined together by lines that run across the plains, in wind, in sun, in storms. Then an ending, an obituary. 'Who died?' people ask at the café-bar or the store when the funeral lights come on, or when they play the recorded bells on LVA, the town's radio station.

It was a Pascualini, one of the ones that lives behind the fire station.

The one they always called Filón.

No, that one's brother. The one who married one of those Pautaso girls from El Molle.

The Pautasos were those four sisters where every single one of them was good-looking?

Right. This guy was married to Delia, one of the middle sisters.

The Pascualini whose boy had that accident.

No, that was the one where the boy got all those oil burns and had to spend a long time in the hospital in Córdoba. This guy would be that boy's uncle. This is the Pascualini that one time when he went on a trip with the folks from the co-op, the escalator ate his sleeve.

The one who had a stroke.

Right, the one who had the stroke.

A look back, and, in the attempt to identify, the narration of an obituary, the drawing that gets created by the tracks of a body over the course of a lot of nights and days. And the times those tracks suddenly switch directions, the afternoons of misfortunes, unexpected incidents, shocks. The Saturday when, for the first time, Pascualini saw one of the Pautaso sisters get out of their cart in front of the church. The Thursday night he felt some discomfort in his left cheek and realized he couldn't move his arm anymore, and then, in an instant, knew that this was how things would be from then on.

I hated those conversations, or I had a phobia or a fear of them. When I heard my family talking about these things, I would open the hallway door, immerse myself in the cold of the unheated part of the house, collapse on my bed, turn on the lamp on my nightstand, open a book, stretch out, and read.

The plot of a novel was a kind of spell, a safeguard against those sketches made up of just some dashes and some wishy-washy lines, vagaries. I needed to lend my own life a fictional shape.

I read because reading was order, harmony, the promise of a third act where everything would come together, where everything would make sense.

I wanted a different kind of life, I guess. I was drawn to the fineness of those far-off, 'smart', perfect places. I was drawn to plots that were so well woven that their finales would assuage all the story's sorrows, prove that all the trials, all the conflicts had been worth it. I wanted a life like the ones I read about in books, a life like the ones in the magazines.

And that desire was the only way I could figure out to tell myself that I wasn't like the others, that I felt different.

Imagining having my own home in that town drove me to despair. Growing old there to the sounds of sowing and threshing.

It wasn't fear of boredom. It was fear of waste.

Escaping to take advantage of the little life a person might get so lucky as to have. That fundamental anxiety: leaving the little town, seeing the world, making the most of life, giving it meaning, as though on its own, simply by occurring, my life didn't have any meaning already.

I felt I had so little time. Time for what? I didn't know, but I was convinced there was another kind of life waiting for me somewhere, and I imagined that I could only really begin to live if I discovered what that place was and what that life was.

So I studied, prepared, tried to get the best grades, learned to be someone else, far away.

I read a lot, read all the time, everything I could get my hands on. I clung to books, to newspapers, to magazines. I absorbed information, assimilated it: anything could be a tool to blaze a trail, to leave, to camouflage myself amongst the locals of anywhere that wasn't Cabrera.

I couldn't understand how the rest of them could live their lives so calmly, how the pampas weren't drowning them, too. I thought I knew so much more than my parents, than my grandparents, than my siblings, than my classmates at school.

None of what was available to me there would be useful. I had to make myself, be my own father, my own mother, leave.

I stopped going out into the countryside and became very serious, very sombre. I was always angry, I spent my weekends reading.

It was really just a need to get everything under control: chaos, meaninglessness, fear.

I thought I was better than everyone, yet I also felt less than.

I didn't know yet, although I had a feeling.

Or I did know, or one day I figured it out, suddenly a suspicion: What if I was into guys? What if I was one of those? No, I couldn't be. Not me. I couldn't be. I wasn't.

The sense of strict secrecy. Not even admitting it to myself so as not to put myself at risk of death.

It would be a great weakness and, above all, I needed to be strong.

Denying it so as not to humiliate my family, not to subject them to shame.

Denying it also so as not to be weak. Proving that I was better than everyone, stronger.

I had very high expectations and put a lot of pressure on myself.

I didn't know how to meet those expectations, I didn't know if I would be able to, I didn't even know if I would have the courage to leave.

Reading warded off the fear: I believed that by identifying all the possible plots, all the possible narrative structures, I would know how to see my own story through to safety.

'If you flee/the around here devours you/if you remain/the around here assimilates you/bestows on you the title of native son,' Elena Anníbali says in a poem.

Honolulu, my dad loved to repeat. Was it the sound of the word? The pleasant repetition of *lu-lu*?
Or was it because it signified a distant, unknown place?
Honolulu.

Had my dad ever dreamt of leaving? Of inventing a new language, made up of pure sounds? A language that had words enough to designate all of its speaker's desires.

I felt I didn't fit in, that I didn't have anyone to talk to, that I would talk, and no one would look at me, that they didn't recognize who I was, that they couldn't see me.

Until the moment when, many years later, I met Ciro, that feeling was always with me.
Not fitting in.
Not having a place.

Long conversations, conversations all the time.
Finding Ciro meant finding someone to talk to, someone with whom to stop being silent.
And it meant finding his body, which got along so well with mine.

Now I have Zapiola, and I have a garden.

It's important to live a complicated life, I read the other day – I'm not sure where, but somewhere, in some magazine.

Cabrera. A sunny day. Cloudless sky. South wind. Very cold. Guadal. Dry. The kind of light that hurts at noon. The broad, deserted streets. Trees cropped low so they won't graze the cables. Wind. Weather. Afternoon light that makes your head hurt.

I go to visit my grandpa's grave, at the Deheza Park Cemetery. The whir of the edible oil refinery can be heard in the distance, barely tempered, but a constant, background noise. Trucks rumble down the highway. The ones on international routes are larger, they travel from Brazil to Chile, they're like lightning, they don't even slow down. The sound of their engines reaches me a little out of sync. First I see them. Then I hear them.

The grass on his grave is patchy. They put down slabs of turf after the burial, but some of them didn't take, and some of them haven't finished stretching out yet. There are some plastic roses in one of the vases in the ground. Below those, a generous handful of the pebbles that cover the main paths and trails. My grandma must have pilfered them to act as ballast, so that the wind doesn't rip up my grandpa's plastic roses and spirit them away to other graves.

I don't really know what to do as I stand there, I read the plaque over and over again: a couple of dates, a phrase I'm sure my grandma chose.

Above, high up, a little falcon shrieks with its wings outstretched. He lets himself be blown around in circles as he keeps perfectly still.

From somewhere comes the buzz of a small plane, but I can't see it anywhere.

On the way back, when I stop for gas, I run into a former high school classmate. He tells me he's separated, that it's been hard on the kids, but that he's dating someone new now.

You don't know her, he tells me. They're not from here, they moved just recently.

You? How've you been? he asks.

Good, good, I say instantly. I've been good, you know, same old.

No one here has ever heard any mention of Ciro.

How could I have thought the light wouldn't hurt my eyes as I was leaving?

In Cabrera, things go back to being called by their original names. Language goes back to being mine.

Flowers scraggle.

Salami isn't salami, it's chorizo, or dry chorizo.

Popcorn is pururú.

Doing laundry is throwing in a bin of washing.

If I go to the butcher's, I no longer need to call cutlets a rib steak or ribs a strip roast, like they do in Buenos Aires.

At the bakery, I can ask for a half pound of criollos, and everyone knows what I'm talking about.

Ways to talk about the time of day:
At nightfall
At siesta hour
Postmeridian
In the dead of night
When the sun comes up
When the sun goes down

At the crack of dawn
At daybreak

Dad watches the Rural Channel, seated at the head of the table. I tell him I'm thinking about writing something about being out in the country, if he can help me with some questions.

What do you need to know?

What it used to be like, when you were young.

Ages ago, he says without taking his eyes off the TV.

He says he isn't sure if he'll remember. That I ought to talk to someone else, someone who would know for sure.

Anything you can tell me, I say.

Papa nods, remains silent, looking at the screen. An agricultural engineer is talking about the cultivation of cassava in some northern province, Salta, Jujuy.

What do you need to know? Dad asks when the agricultural engineer finishes, and the commercial break begins.

How old were you when you started working the fields? I ask him.

Thirteen, fourteen I must have been. I went to boarding school for a year, but they kicked me out of there pretty fast.

What year was that?

Well I was born in '42, so that means '55, '56.

Who was president?

Dad's not sure.

I don't remember... There were so many presidents, I...

Back when it was Frondizi, do you remember what it was like?

Frondizi, Frondizi. I mean, it wasn't bad. But I can't tell you exactly like you'd put in a book, Dad says. I'm

trying to think who could really talk to you about that…
Grandpa could have told you for sure.

It doesn't matter, whatever you remember.

I'm just trying to think who can really tell you. Let me see. We'd need to come up with someone older than me, someone who remembers.

Just anything you feel like you can tell me, I say. When you started working, for example, what was being planted then?

Wheat, flax, corn. There were many more cows than what they've got now, lots and lots of cows. There was a fair every Friday.

But there wasn't any soy yet.

No, soy came later, says Dad.

On the Rural Channel now, the commercials have ended. The programme starts again. Agricultural machines, seeders, disc harrows. Dad turns, crosses his arms, looks at the screen in silence.

We decide to go out for a drive.

I heard the Fesia boy bought a new car, a Toyota, white, Dad says. Go that way, so we pass by their house, let's see if it's outside.

I turn the wheel.

No, no, the other way, Dad says.

But don't the Fesias live on the boulevard?

No, the oldest son, I mean, the one that married the Gastaudo girl. They rented Oscar Macagno's house, over there by that canal.

I nod. I drive slowly. Dad gets nervous if we put the car in anything but second gear.

We drive up in front of Macagno's house. Everything's shut, dark.

This is the place, Dad says, but no, I guess they didn't take the car out today.

We keep going toward the neighbourhood of La Polenta.

Take this road, Papa says, pointing to some lots dotted with new houses.

The town is growing quite a bit on this end, more and more, says Dad. They're building a lot of houses. I think this one belongs to one of the Actis kids, and that one there to Puchulino's son. The town is getting big. I heard Mary Gómez opened up a business, let's see, wait, go around the block. Dad points to a garage with an awning out in front.

That must be it, he shows me. I heard she put in a little store there.

We take the new highway that goes to Gigena in order to see if a storm is coming. At the entrance to the town, not long ago, they built a ramp and an embankment, at the place where the two highways intersect. Since its inauguration, that's where all the old Italians go in the evenings to look at the sky, because from that height, you can see farther.

We ascend the ramp slowly. From the top of the bridge, we see a field of soybeans that have already been harvested, dotted here and there with plastic bags the wind has blown over from the dump. Dad looks at the horizon. He says there's a storm brewing, that it'll be a big one.

I look, and I don't see anything.

Yep, says Dad. Quite the storm.

Life in the country consists of looking. Looking at the slightly greyish, opulent band that rises over the horizon and knowing whether it's rain coming or just some clouds. Looking at the halos that show off the moon. Seeing if the sun goes down neat or not.

Here no one thinks in satellite images, but in clouds that could come closer or move farther away, in signs from the sky, minimal shifts. Nature's language consists of recurrences. Learning to read that language involves knowing how to stop, take note, recognize, look closely.

So, I say, soybeans. When did the soybeans make it over here?

You mean what year? I couldn't tell you that, Dad says.

Well, who first brought them in?

The Oil Plant, says Dad. Ñoño went to the U.S. and came back with three, four hundred bags and gave them out to all the Italians. He gave Cerutti forty, Perticarari forty, Malatini forty. That's how the soybean came to be here, in this region.

Did he give our family some?

He offered it to us, but Grandpa didn't want it at first. Uncle Bauta did, he started up with it right away. We didn't get going till three or four years later. The first round was in the field with the iron gate. There were thirty-three hectares, and he gave us thirty quintals.

I nod, Dad nods. We're sitting in the truck, on the bridge, at the intersection of the two-lane highways. The engine is running, but the truck's in neutral. Just in case, I'm pressing my right foot down on the brake. Dad looks back toward the storm. The light is getting orange, pink. It tinges the windshield, dyes his skin, his pupils.

Uncle Bauta came one morning and set up the machine for us. He told us how many kilos of seed to put in, the kilos, the depth, everything, Dad says. Uncle Bauta had got the hang of it by that time, he'd been planting it for three or four years already. He came that day and showed us how to do it, and then the very next day it rained a shit ton, sixty millimetres out of the blue.

I nod again. I imagine that that much rain after sowing isn't good, but I don't really know why. I don't know this story. I've never heard it before.

The problem with soy is that if you plant it too deep, and it rains, since the ground will be loose, the seed will sink, and then the soil will form a crust over it, and you'll be fucked, you'll just never see it, Dad says. So right then Uncle Bauta came back. He took a good look and told me: Get the harrow ready. We got out the Deutz 730, which had the narrowest wheel, and we harrowed the whole field. Wherever the wheels passed over, the soy wouldn't come up, the weight broke the beans. Those tracks stayed like they were set in stone, but the rest of it came up fine. So even with everything that happened we got thirty quintals out of it. It was the Gu and the Pla, those were the first kinds of soy planted here, the ones Ñoño had brought in the seeds for.

Thirty quintals is good, I say.

It is good, Dad says. For that time it was good, anyway. Just think, there weren't any sprays or fertilizers then, nothing. Thirty quintals was great.

Then he takes a breath, rolls down his window a little, tells me to put the truck in first.

At that time, we would plant the soy and weed it with a hoe, he says, and then we'd go through and finish the job by hand. We didn't even have fumigators. After about four or five years we bought a Venini that was a piece of junk. And after that we bought a fumigator in Hernando. A square one, orange in colour, flimsy, but it worked. It was then, when Roundup came out, that things really got going.

What year was that in?

Dad shrugs.

I really don't remember, he says. The first people who sold Roundup around here were Arsenio Morichetti and Franchisqueti, the agricultural engineer. He was the engineer, so he was the one who explained all these things to us. You had to put the Roundup into the land once it was ploughed, and the harrow went behind it to stir up the earth a little, for everything to mix. Before you planted, you put in Roundup. It was a crazy thing we were doing. You'd work the land with a ploughshare, then a multimodal before planting, then you'd spray the Roundup, and then you'd harrow it and beat down the ground, to firm it, because the soy wouldn't come up in loose soil. Or it would come up, but then it would rain, and that would send your seeds down. The good thing about Roundup was that it killed everything, so you didn't need to weed anymore.

And did it make things better? I ask. Did your yields go up?

Oh, they went up, Dad says. But besides that it was less work, less costly. Then again, Roundup doesn't have the same effect as it used to. After thirty years, the plants are all saturated with Roundup, they're resistant. Nothing you can do. We keep having to put in new treatments. That's a truckload of money.

Slowly we go back into town, passing in front of the hangar that the Pitavinos, the town's wealthiest family, are building for their helicopters. The Pitavinos are four brothers who started off with fifty hectares to work, renting fifty more from a bachelor uncle. All soy. Year after year. Now they own almost six thousand hectares – or so people say. They've bought up fields in the north, in Salta, in Bolivia. They rent all over the place. They bought an entire block of the town, and each brother built a gigantic house on each corner, and they had a pool and a barbecue area done in the middle, to be shared.

Dad tells me it's in fashion now to inspect the fields by helicopter. There's no longer time for ground transportation. These are important people, they care about their time. They look at the clouds from above.

The problem is that each of them wants to have more than the others, says Dad. And the sisters-in-law fight about who gets to use the pool.

Then he suggests we go buy chorizos from a woman in Carnerillo.

He says she makes them just like they did in the old days.

It can be treacherous to climb a mountain, because mountains 'are completely inhospitable, and it is extremely difficult to navigate by stones and snow,' says Jorge Leónidas Escudero. 'But the mountain is sacred. And in the mountains, we can sense communication from the whole, the all-encompassing. The luminous, we don't know if it's God or what it is. A tremendous thing that is beyond us, and here we are in it. The inhospitable nature of the mountain gives us the feeling that we belong to a whole that is beyond our ephemeral life.'

God is always on high. In the Old Testament, wherever there is a mountain, that's where God is to be found.

On the summits, clouds cover peaks. That's the place to meet with God: in the clouds, in the fog.

Those who live on the plains live with the knowledge that God is far away, live looking up.

The plains, the pampas, are also the absence of height. No point from which to survey the land. No point from which to look down, to look over.

Life on the plains, without the possibility of getting out, without heights to climb to find the sacred.

In Exodus, God is the cloud. He guides the way, offers shade in the desert.

A perfect blue sky, without a single trace of white.

Once the Israelites reached the promised land, manna stopped falling from heaven. God no longer appeared in the form of burning bushes, God was no longer fire. The clouds became just clouds, God was no longer hiding in them. The clouds suddenly meant nothing, they no longer told of anything.

The careful Father had become an elusive God, difficult to see. A God without signs, a God in absentia.

How can we read something that doesn't have any letters in it? How do we go on, how are we supposed to proceed in the complete absence of signs? How can we continue without a Father who will tell us how?

A God without signs is almost a non-existent God. We are at his mercy, we cannot go looking for him, only he can approach if he wants to…; the rest is faith.

The mountain as the place where we are close to God and from where we can see others in a kind of wide shot, from above, in a high or semi-high angle shot, a bird's-eye shot over the valley.

In the pampas, we can't see our neighbours. We don't have the height to gain sufficient distance.

Horizontality. The pampas as the place where we are lost.

I tried to tell my mum once.

No, she said.

Her face had darkened.

No, she said, and I never really knew what that negation meant.

It's not true.

I won't allow it.

I don't believe that.

I don't want to know.

Don't say it.

I can't.

After that, it was never spoken of. If I brought up the subject, it was as though that part fell on deaf ears. Silence. Talk about something else, change the subject.

I have lunch with my grandmother. She's doing well, she's lucid. She is ninety-one years old, but she's continuing to live the same life she always has. A couple of months after Grandpa died, we obliged her to move into town. It was impossible for someone her age to live alone in the countryside. Now she keeps her vegetable garden between mudwalls, small, but lovely. From the country she brought the lilies and the irises and the gladiolus bulbs; all she sows is chard, chicory, and lettuce, what she eats and what's easy. Green and yellow squash, in the summer. And some tomato and pepper plants.

You didn't put in any cabbage? I ask her as I take out a few weeds and water a little.

Nah, what's the point, she says. It's easier to get it at the greengrocer's.

She bakes some meat, some golden potatoes like only she can make. Later, while she offers me coffee over and over again, and over and over again I tell her I don't want any, I ask her about the box of old photos, if I can keep some, if she still has them.

Of course, she says, and goes to look for it in her room.

The box is the same as always, same flowers on the fabric, same disorder of loose photos. I look at them a while and choose three or four, my favourites, almost all of them photos of the Giraudo uncles: dressed as gunfighters, posing next to a newly bought car, on a trip, in Rosario, in front of the monument to the flag.

When I flip them over, I discover something new: on the back of each photo, on the cardstock on the back, my grandmother has written in neat handwriting the name of the person who appears in the image, a short description, a tentative date.

What's this? I ask her.

So that when I'm gone, you all won't forget, she says. So you have it.

I nod, not knowing how to respond.

I rummage through the box, look at more photos, look at the image, read the back. Grandma starts setting the table. I find a photo of her, from her wedding day. Grandfather was a jolly, chubby man, with a receding hairline already and very little hair, even though he had only just returned from doing his military service. She's wearing a white dress, a wide skirt. They got married in Punta del Agua, on a very windy day. The wind rumples her dress, sends up her veil.

What about this one? I ask. Can I take it?

No, not that one, says Grandma. If you want, you can go right here to the kiosk and make a photocopy if you like, but that one stays with me.

My grandmother, sitting at the head of the table, with the box of photos next to her, has taken them all out and, one by one, on the back of each photo, she writes down who's in them, the approximate year, and the summary of an anecdote. Her elongated handwriting, writing names, surnames in straight lines, what they did, when, with whom, to keep us from forgetting them.

How to write from a landscape with no past, with no history?

A landscape conceived of as empty requires stories to cover it, to fill it up.

It requires telling these stories, over and over, to yourself, and to others, in order not to plummet into meaninglessness.

The history of those who have tried to fill that void, prolix, written in her handwriting: years, marriages, baptisms.

She is the one who passes the baton of memory.

The pampas are harsh and demanding terrain, not at all bucolic. Black night. Tough land. The wind. The wind. The heat of the sun without shade. Without relief. The grandeur, the thistled ground, the epochs of thistles. The salt in the dried soil of the swamp. Salt in your face. The constant filth, the discomfort of the body, frozen water in winter, the soil in summer, floods, rocks, droughts, caterpillar infestations, locusts, the storms that pass by, the moisture that doesn't come. The plains are hard, the countryside is cruel, it does not necessarily offer any comfort.

The stories of the dead, covering the soybean plains.

It works by contrast.

Writing about the empty pampa is also writing about milestones, surveyors, prices, values, the need for someone to cut out, for someone to measure.

It's writing about meetings, negotiations, bribes, returning favours, notaries, ID cards, papers.

Property titles, lot by lot. The patriarchal line. The pater familias. Inheritance.

In cutting out the void, the illusion that the void has disappeared.

Pampas. In the cutting, in the moulding, in the gridding, the desire to possess.

This is mine, said the first Juan.

This is yours, he told his son.

The terror of beholding the pampas: Does this explain the religiosity, the clinging to God once a person has been exposed to the elements?

That and the only discourse that fills and gives meaning around these parts is that of God the Father.

The church bell tower: the tallest building. The only thing that can be seen from afar.

The priest as the only person we tell certain things we feel, things we don't know how to put into words, things we carry inside us.

The priest listens, blesses.

'Patience,' says the priest.

'Prudence,' says the priest.

Time is treacherous on the plains. The round dances of the harvest. We have the sense that time is not passing, that everything is coming up again to start afresh, we have the sense that we aren't getting any older.

The emptiness is productive. It gets filled up with crops.

The song of the harvests is long, mysterious. It's hard to identify its rhythm, if it has one.

It takes a long time to uncover its beat, it takes a lifetime to learn to dance to its music.

The music of the harvests is a spell it can be hard to snap out of.

Fear of the horizon.

Fear of emptiness, of meaninglessness, of routine. To drop dead one morning crossing the square and not have anything in your hands to barter with.

Is that why I went far away from this horizon?

Is that why I surround myself with horizon now, again?

Immigrants who come from mountain towns and are now lost in the pampas.

Immigrants who miss the mountains and in the face of this emptiness die by suicide, throwing themselves into the well. They hang themselves because they believe the war is coming back, or because they believe themselves lost.

The pampas also forces you to face that almost Zen truth: there is no better place to ascend to, no happiness to achieve, nowhere to go, nothing to reach.

This is it, and this will always be it.

Some can peer into the void. Others get vertigo.

It might force you to accept it, or give you wisdom,
or make you desperate,
or resigned.

The difference between resignation and surrender.

The difference between accepting and knowing how to let go.

The difference between always being silent and having nothing to say.

The difference between wisdom and anaesthesia.

A terrifying fear, a fear of death, a paralyzing fear, that day, as he drove around with his father. If he told him, he would completely cease to exist for him, he knows. But he has to do it. His throat is dry, his hands tremble.

The father listens, says nothing.

Are you going to come back to Cabrera someday? Are you going to come back and live here? he asks.

No, I don't think so.

So then do whatever you want, you'd know best, says the father. But don't even think about coming into town with some guy, don't even think about discussing it in town, what would be the point, besides, what business is it of theirs.

Then they stop in front of the house, and the father gets out, and the son drives on.

I head back. The same rosary of towns, but in reverse. Deheza, Perdices, Dalmacio. Finally Villa María, the highway.

Little by little I stop being who I am in the little town and, as the car moves forward, I return to being who I am in Buenos Aires.

One self in the town.

Another self outside it.

It takes me a long time to remember that I am no longer returning to our house, to the house I built with Ciro, to what felt to me like a family.

Who I am in Buenos Aires is changing, mutating, something broke, and nothing new has come yet to replace it.

I cry a while and think of Ciro.

Do I still miss him?

Yes, of course. I still miss him. It still hurts, I have to make an effort almost every day, try and keep up my spirits, try and keep my mind off him.

Once, a long time ago, I met a girl who, as soon as she graduated from college, went into a frenzy of travel, of nomadism that lasted almost fifteen years: She began in Brazil, then Spain, giving massages on the beach, selling bikinis. In Italy, she worked in a bar while her application for citizenship was being processed. Then India, Malaysia, Italy again, England for a while, Spain again.

She told me that of all those minimal homes she made along the way, what she liked most of all was that in each place she could be someone different. Invent herself a new life each time she made new friends. Add or subtract siblings, twist her history, invent a happy childhood rambling in hills, a happy childhood in an apartment, a very sad childhood on a fishing boat, a childhood cut short by an accident involving a rock, whatever.

In each place, talk about the father, the mother, the mother's father, the father's mother, the neighbours, the house, the neighbourhood, the landscape in a different way, and therefore, be a different person.

I'm used to being someone different in the different worlds I live in: talking to some people about heifers and crops, while with others, books and poetry, with others contemporary art or cinema, or flowers, tomatoes, seeds, or love and gossip, with other friends.

But sometimes, a lot of the time, I wish I could always be the same.

Be the same in the town, the same in the city, the same in the country, the same when I kiss, the same when I yearn, the same sowing seeds in the garden, the same when I write.

And sometimes it seems to me that I am closest to achieving that when I'm driving alone on the road, at seventy-five miles per hour, suspended in that motion, between the city and the fields, floating over the crops, over the soy that, under the sun, undulates in the wind.

Telling a story changes the person who tells it.

And sometimes, fiction is the only way to think about what's true.

JUNE

That fear in my hands on the steering wheel when I enter Buenos Aires. That trembling. The body that shakes. What am I doing, what is this. It's insane. My stomach contracts, my hands clench. Wanting to retreat, forget, abandon, but making myself go forward, because everything's going to be okay, everything's going to be okay.

The speed of the other cars. A truck glued to my bumper, forcing me to speed up, to go faster and faster. I try to move over so he can pass, but the next lane is solid with cars. Without knowing how, I ended up in the fast lane, now I can't switch.

Zarate, Campana, Escobar. Maxiconsumo Marolio. A truck that's blown a tyre, roadside assistance approaching. More posters. Quintas. Footbridges. Towers of lights and antennas. Piero: the best mattress. Gaucho: clothing that will stand up to anything. From time to time, rows of trees. Out of the corner of my eye, I see that in every single row, there's one tree missing, a tree that has fallen, or that hasn't grown, or that the wind has knocked down, row interrupted. My car is packed to the brim: trunk full of boxes of books, nightstands, clothes in black plastic bags, lamps, a chair in the backseat, blankets, a comforter, boxes of dishes wrapped in newspaper.

The Panamericana highway. Two lanes. Four lanes. Six lanes. All full of cars. All going at maximum velocity. Being forced into the flow. Forced to keep going. The current that drags along. No going back. This is it. I can't stop, I'm in it now.

Sawmills.

Construction yards.

Service stations.

Parking lots with cars parked in the sun.

Furniture stores.

Houses behind fences. Gated communities.

A toll, the highway rising. The houses below are little, low. You can see their roofs, the dirty streets that run in front of them, stagnant water in the gutters.

Huge advertising hoardings.

Tanks, cisterns. Half-finished buildings. Dingy terraces.

A crashed car on top of a column. A warning to wear your seatbelt.

General Paz. I didn't have GPS, back then there was no Waze, or Google Maps. Throughout my journey I'd been repeating to myself, until learning by heart, which exit to take to enter the city, to finally be free of the freeway. You flick the indicator, and you turn left. Pull over on the first quiet street you come to, call Ciro. His voice on speaker, telling me every traffic light, every street, what I was going to see on the corner, how far I had to go, where I had to turn.

A few days before he'd tested the route on his bicycle and, in order to be able to guide me, written everything down on a yellow notepad. He read these notes to me slowly, asking me whether or not I had already seen the sign for that painters' shop, the façade of a house that was covered in brown tiles, a block of cobblestones and tall plane trees. Driving to Ciro's while listening to the sound of his voice. Him waiting for me at the door. Only once he saw me did he take the phone away from his ear and slip it into his pocket.

Welcome, he said.

I go back to Zapiola. I find the garden in good shape, lovely, progressing. Luiso has been watering it in my absence. Lots of weeds. The broad beans are growing at a good pace. The cabbage has already sent out big, broad leaves. Only the chard is a bit stagnant, or not as leafy as I imagined it would be.

The peas, too, didn't do too much. They stayed as they were, tiny. I thought they might be able to face the winter a little more grown, but they've only put out a couple of thin shoots, little leaves dotted with specks, as if infested or mildewed. Maybe I planted them too late, the ground was already cold.

The chinaberry trees are very yellow. They really stand out now. The oak leaves have turned a deep, coppery red.

One of the chickens is missing. I ask Luiso, who I'd left in charge of feeding them and making sure they had water.

She was sick a couple of days, he says, and I took her home with me so she wouldn't infect the others. She died there, at my place. It must have been some type of virus, because she wasn't pecked or anything, she just didn't want to eat.

I nod. I feel sad, but these kinds of things happen

sometimes. Especially with this type of laying hen, which has a reputation for being delicate.

What's new in town? I ask him.

Nothing, nothing I know of, says Luiso.

The sun sets at half past five. By six, it's dark.

Sadness of winter in the countryside.

Long winter nights in the countryside.

Although it doesn't quite get down to freezing, it's the first day and first week of real cold.

I turn on the woodstove. I find a dead bird in the ash box. It must have flown into the chimney in the summer and not been able to find its way back out.

The house changes. The arrangement of the furniture changes. Everything now revolves around the stove.

Rubbing my hands together every time I come in, trying to get rid of the cold from my body, moving closer to the stove, spreading my fingers out over the iron.

The smell of a tangerine has permeated my nails. Walking into town under the midday sun, eating the segments one at a time and letting the peel fall over my tracks like breadcrumbs or signals for who knows whom, for no one, to follow me.

The acacias have lost their leaves. They only have their black pods left, long and dry, hanging twisted in on themselves and filled with seeds. They clatter with the wind.

A frog in the bathtub. Frogs sleeping pressed together in the soil of the vegetable bed.

Bonnard: 'I am an old man now, and I begin to see

that I do not know any more than I knew when I was young.' I read that in a book about his work.

Damp cold, cloudy. The yellow of the chinaberry trees contrasting with the leaden sky. How hard it is to wake up in winter. Unwillingness, sloth. Body stiffened by cold. Coming out from under the sheets. Getting dressed. Stove off. Going outside to turn on the pump, filling it with water. Putting on the coffee. Splashing your face with the cold water the tap coughs out. Teeth chattering, lips quivering, a stinging running down your spine. Making a little bowl of water out of your very white, almost blue fingers. Washing your eyes out, brushing off the margins of your eyelids, dragging out the sleep, pressing your hair down, wetting the back of your neck, wiping just a little water under your armpits. Drying off fast. Body still numb, rigid.

The day begins.

Hibernation time. Time to stay still and not do anything, let growth be underneath, like the roots of a tree, on the inside.

Cabbage-like, as the Chileans say. 'You're all cabbage-like': you're inward, rolled up around yourself, growing solo, pressed up against your thoughts.

'The love encounter between two people is the rapport between their childhoods,' say Kristeva and Sollers.

Ciro lying on his bed, reading one of my books, while I write, sitting at his table. At some point, I see him rest the book on his chest, grab his phone, and write something.

My cell phone dings. An email from Ciro: 'there's a city growing inside me that's named after you. Fede Town. It has squares, buildings, bridges, bicycles, terraces... Each of your books adds more and more images to it and gives me vertigo.'

In the emptiness of the plains. Suddenly, the construction of a town.

He was born and had always lived in the big city, but his father's family was from a small town in the province of Santa Fe. When he was a teenager, he spent many of his summers there, going with his grandfather to the countryside, he had many cousins, and he was always going to visit them.

He told me about it little by little, in our conversations while we were cooking, or as we went to the market, on Saturday mornings, or as we walked around Buenos Aires, on Sundays.

He was from Buenos Aires, but he knew all about riding his bike with a band of friends in the siesta hour through a bare and empty town, he knew about the sticky heat of summer nights drinking beer on the square or by the community pool, he knew about roasting suckling pigs at Christmas, about stealing peaches and jumping over walls, about eating plums straight from the tree and getting rid of warts with the droplet of milk that comes out when you pluck a fig. He knew, he understood that landscape that I, in order to be able to be myself, had left behind, that I had turned my back on, that I had lost.

He never concealed the fact that he liked boys. I could picture it: the cousin from Buenos Aires, the little scandal of the town, admiration and fear intermingled. Every December he'd arrive with the latest information: what clothes they were supposed to be wearing, how to wear their hair, the myriad anecdotes from parties he had gone to, celebrities he'd seen. In his bag he carried cassettes recorded off the radio, indie bands that he knew of when nobody else did yet, and that he'd have them listen to on the tape player in their grandfather's car while they drove around and around, on Saturday afternoons, the eldest cousin behind the wheel, elbows out, the windows open to let the air flow through.

I could picture it, see it through the eyes of the village kids: the first earring anyone had ever seen in the distant confines of the provinces, the first tongue piercing, the first boy with dyed hair at the end of the year he decided to turn goth and sport black hair, the calls from that first boyfriend he'd left behind in Buenos Aires, answered sitting on the floor, next to the telephone, his fingers playing with the cord, unrolling it and rolling it back up, the backwards baseball caps, the scraped knees, the borrowed bicycle, the breath that smelled of beer, picking off scabs and eating them sitting on the sidewalk, the girls who fell madly in love with him because he was unattainable, beautiful, and from the capital.

I could picture it, every morning, when I watched him get out of bed with his sleepy face, or as he was preparing mate, smelling his body, when I went around his house, the books on his shelves, the neat order of the drawers where he kept his underwear, the little refuge he'd built, an old, long apartment on the second floor, positioned above all the other homes on his block, the home into which he was inviting me now.

It was as though I'd known him in another life, as though our childhoods complemented one another, as though absolutely nothing needed to be said because everything had always already been made clear.

I pull weeds and create some little drainage ditches. Quick lunch and very brief nap. I'm awakened by the wind: mosquito curtain strips slamming against the kitchen door. Outside the temperature has dropped even more. I read in front of the woodstove. At times the sun peeks out, but most of the time it's cloudy. Cold and windy. At dusk, I go for a walk. I walk up to the little hill with the poplars. The ones that are deep inside only have a few leaves left. The caracaras are already beginning to settle into the branches of the acacia trees to spend the night. The chimangos circle. Proliferation of ducks in the marsh. They take flight as soon as I get close. A guinea pig runs across the road. I go back. Omelette with chard and finely chopped kale. Also cream of pea soup, from a packet.

The sound at night on entering the house. The curtain strips. The wooden door. That same combination of sounds that, in my childhood, in the countryside of my grandparents, the doors that led to the backyard, to the laundry room, made. The silence of being inside.

The crackling of the embers in the woodstove, in back of the iron.

The dream of one day having a wood-burning stove in the kitchen.

The pleasure of sleeping under lots of blankets, of weight pressing down on my body.

Yellow chinaberry leaves strewn across the freshly hoed soil of the new bed.

So-called 'oxheart' cabbage: I don't know if it's called that because of how good and faithful oxen are or because it is supposed to form a sharp little head.

The house in the foreground at dusk, the golden colours of the last winter light.

Then it rains, and the chinaberry trees are stripped completely.

I'm awakened by thunderclaps, bolts of lightning darting in through the cracks in the window, flashes that turn the whole sky white. Storm. Bucketfuls of rain. Strong, swirling wind. In the darkness I hear shouting. I fumble with the knob of the lamp on my nightstand, but the electricity has gone out. I get up and feel my way into the kitchen. In the dead of the night, rain lashing the trees, the roof, the walls of the house. The noise on the zinc roof is overwhelming, but here and there, between the gusts and gusts of wind, I think I can distinguish – outside, far, shouting – the voice of my neighbour, his curses. My flashlight is on the first shelf of the cupboard, next to the glasses and cups, in a corner. I turn it on and point it down, just at the floor, a small circle of light on the tiles. I go up to the desk, turn off the flashlight. Barefoot, I peer out the window, trying to see what's going on.

Through the rain that runs down the glass, I see the neighbour's truck, straddling the road, with its headlights shining into my garden. My neighbour is a dark shadow, with stooped shoulders, who comes and goes, runs and passes in front of the headlights, slips, shouts, falls, gets up, keeps going. The rain drips down his chin, through his hair, splashes, bursts onto his shoulders, his back. At first I don't get what he's doing. Another fit of rage? Then, the screech of a pig, and a shadow that darts in front of the headlights. It looks like he bucks, like he raises his hindquarters, kicks. Behind, my neighbour trying to grab him, running with his arms outstretched. Suddenly I understand: the pigs have escaped. My heart contracts, my chest tightens. They're going to destroy everything, my beds, the cabbage, the chard. I hear them shrieking as they're chased. My neighbour comes and goes. I'm about to go out, but I stop myself. What am I going to do? What can I do? Try to scare them off? After a while, my neighbour gets into the truck, reverses, turns and his headlights fill my eyes, blind me as they light up the whole façade of the house. Out of pure instinct, I crouch down, even though I know that, from that distance and in the rain, it isn't possible for him to see me. The truck lights up the brick walls of one of his sheds, but only for an instant. He starts moving again, perpendicular to me now. Then I can see the two red lights on the back of the truck. He accelerates, goes around the sheds, gets lost behind them, moving away to where his pens are. Silence. Now only the rain remains, and even the rain seems to fall more calmly. It takes me a long time to go back to bed. Only when I lie down do I realize that my legs and my arms are shaking, that my feet are freezing cold.

I can't get to sleep, I barely doze off, lost in thoughts that become tangled, strange, illogical, waking dreams.

I put on my rubber boots and go out to investigate at dawn, gloomy, blue, very wet. It's not raining anymore, just an occasional drizzle.

Some damage, but not much, in the garden. The pigs rooted in the onion furrow, crushed the lettuce, a little bit the chard, trampled part of the broad bean bed. The worst damage is to the new bed, but there isn't anything planted there yet, so that's not a problem, I just rake out the soil and level it again. Otherwise, everything is very green and damp. A broccoli plant, the tallest one, tilted by the wind, almost fallen; I will have to give it some supports. Lots of mud on the road.

Another chicken dead after the storm. I find her in the middle of a puddle, her feet yellow, pale, as though washed, stretched out backwards, the three calloused toes pressed in on themselves, closed like a cocoon. I don't understand what she's doing there. Why didn't she stay inside? Her feathers are all wet, dripping with water, stuck to her body. She looks emaciated. You can't see the head, it's under the brown water, buried in the puddle, submerged. As though she had fallen in headfirst, despite the fact that the puddle is shallow, can't be more than three centimetres deep.

The two remaining chickens scratch at the mud, just next to her but without paying her any mind. I pick up the dead chicken by the legs. It's like touching the body of a toad, but hardened.

I cross the back field with the dead chicken hanging at my side. I hold her by the legs, dragging her beak over the bright green grass that is saturated with water. When I reach the fence, I spin her around in the air and throw her as far as I can, into the marsh. She falls with a dull thud and is lost among the shepherd's needles, the tamarinds, the common horsetail.

Luiso finds me in the garden, trying to get my beds in order. It's not raining anymore, and he stays a minute, watching me. From his shirt pocket he takes a cigarette and lights it.

Shouldn't be doing that now, he tells me. You ought

to wait for it to air out. If you move the soil around now you're just going to create clods.

I tell him about the pigs, about the onions, the lettuce.

What was he doing here at night? Luiso asks. Is he spending the night here now? Is he not going back to Lobos?

I shrug. I tell him I don't know.

What time would it have been, when you saw him? Luiso asks me.

Four something, almost five.

Could he have come to live here now? Could my sister finally have thrown him out? he asks.

I don't know what to tell him. I begin attaching the fallen broccoli plant to the cane I've driven in beside it.

You better let him know, Luiso says. Go over and explain to him he can't just let his pigs loose like that. They wreck everything, they'll ruin your whole thing here.

He didn't let them loose, I say. They got away from him.

He lets them loose, Luiso insists. I know what I'm talking about. Their hooves get all messed up from being penned in all the time, and then he lets them out for a few days until they heal.

But Luiso, what would he be doing at four-thirty in the morning, putting them back in their pens? They got away from him.

You better let him know, Luiso repeats. He can't get away with it. Otherwise tomorrow you'll find ten piglets at your place. I know what I'm talking about, this guy doesn't give a shit about anything.

Luiso insists so much that, in the end, I cross the road and go to have a word with the neighbour. The yard in front of the sheds, full of puddles, a hopper without wheels resting on four logs, piles of old batteries, rusty drums. I bang on the gate and dogs bark inside, but they don't come out. They're locked inside the shed, I hear them scraping their paws against the metal gate. I knock again, again the dogs bark.

Hello? I say and wait a while. I turn around.

As though pretending to have no idea what's going on, Luiso has gone over to his little shed and is acting like he's working on something, but in reality, he's watching me. With a gesture of his hand, he indicates that I should go on, that I should continue.

Hello? I say again, and again I bang on the gate.

Through the crack under the metal gate I can see the dogs' snouts, sticking out, sniffing my scent in the air. Next to the gate there's a half-open, dilapidated door. I barely touch it, and it opens. Inside is just a single tumbledown room, with a single window. The plaster has fallen off the walls, and the floor is covered in grit. In one corner I see an old box spring on the floor, a twin-size mattress on top of it, with no sheets but with a pillow and a jumble of blankets. Next to it, up by the headboard, some rubber boots covered in still-wet mud, a battery-powered radio, a bottle-top stove. And hanging from a nail, on one of the walls, a hanger with a light blue shirt, clean, ironed.

Hello? Anyone here?

All I can hear is the dogs barking. I close the door and slowly walk away.

He's not there, there's no one there, I tell Luiso when I get back to my garden.

I don't tell him about the blankets, the heater, the shirt. I don't say anything more.

I hope my sister's thrown that piece of shit out for good, Luiso says regardless.

Emotions are never words. They are rather a dynamic superposition of gases that are revealed little by little, overlapping, replacing each other, becoming liquid when they meet, crystallizing into old pains, loves laid to rest.

Language works for perceptions, for everything that enters through the skin, for the shrewdness of the five senses, but emotions always manage to elude it. Words fail them, or tend to fail them, or aren't enough for what we feel within ourselves, in the space between mind and flesh.

Those first months, those first years, even, when I would suddenly look up and find him there, eating on the other side of the table, or washing the dishes, or reading lying on the couch I'd still wonder: Who is this stranger? How can I trust this person to this extent? What is he hiding from me? When is this going to end?

Those first months, those first years, when, suddenly, I'd look up and around, I still couldn't believe that all of it was real. The great joy, the happiness that suddenly hit me, when I stepped back just a little from everyday life and could look. What luck, to wind up in such circumstances! What a privilege, what joy, to have ended up like this, to have trusted, to have worked up the courage to get on the highway, to let myself be dragged along between the other cars, to let myself get carried away.

'Eventually soulmates meet, for they have the same hiding place.' Just that phrase, in English, Ciro sent me one day, in an email. I was writing, lying on the couch, my laptop on my lap. He was supposedly working, sitting at his desk, five metres away.

I love you, I said and turned my head slightly, searching for him with my eyes.

Me too. Leave me alone, he responded without raising his hands from the keyboard or turning to look back.

His mattress was very old, very uncomfortable, full of rickety springs that formed holes or that jumped out, pushing the canvas fabric, creating speedbumps, rises, lumps on the surface. Ciro always slept in the same position and on the same side, the springs had already absorbed the imprint of his body, and they didn't bother him, but for me it was impossible to sleep on that mattress, so that in general I preferred to return to my apartment. My box spring was new, good, soft. On weekends he came to sleep with me.

We would cook at his house, because the kitchen was more comfortable and better equipped. We slept in mine. I had already moved, I had my own apartment. We lived in the same neighbourhood, a block and a half from each other. We came and went all day. We both knew by heart, tile by tile, those one hundred and fifty metres, exactly three minutes, four hundred and thirty-four steps.

Ciro always made the same joke: he didn't get rid of the mattress because if he had, I would have moved in for real, and he would never have been able to get rid of me.

Like most of his jokes, it was his way of saying things he couldn't or didn't know how to say any other way. I got the message, but at the same time, I didn't get it. There were always doubts about the foundations of the joke: Was he saying it for real, was it a warning, a keep your distance? Was it just a way of putting a certain tension into words, of gaining control over it, giving it some space? Or maybe it was just a way to laugh at ourselves, and it meant nothing?

Sometimes that obsession with unsaid or half-said things would lodge itself in my mind and start bouncing around and turning circles until it turned into my being overwhelmed, or exhausted, or sad.

But then, nothing went wrong: Ciro was there, he wanted to be there, our relationship continued, we found places where we could talk, where we could laugh, what mattered was the day to day.

Little by little I learned not to pay attention to his hints. To hear them just as something that had to be said but that generated no consequences. I learned also to intuit his fears, what he kept hushed and how to read between his lines, what he was making an effort to get over. We were both still getting to know each other, groping blindly forward, we didn't want to be overconfident or get hurt.

We played that game all the time: I would come closer, Ciro would retreat two steps. Affectionate boundaries as soon as he saw I was getting too close. His distance made me anxious, I'd give it to him but be filled with worries. Then he'd reconsider, say something, he had his move: he'd call.

Once, at dinner, I overheard a conversation Ciro was having, a little ways away, with a friend.

'A neurotic always needs a safe place to hide,' she told him.

Some nights, when I walked back to my apartment alone, deep down, very deep, I found myself thinking:

Where am I going to find someone else like him? If he doesn't love me, who could?

I was surprised to find myself like this: What was this new fear? Where had it come from? Who was this new me? Where was the person who could go it alone, the one who didn't have any needs, the one who was going to go far, far away and prove to everyone that he was good just like that, on his own?

Was it love that had transformed me so extensively?

Over the years, over the months, I got used to that inhale, exhale in the way, in the manner we loved each other.

A dynamic balance between my anxieties and his phobias.

My fear of being alone, my fear of losing him.

His fear of being trapped, his fear of being loved and then not being loved anymore.

I was always convincing myself: Why should it be easy, when finding someone is so hard?

This is the way you build a real relationship, a serious relationship, I told myself.

It's work, you have to be patient.

The fear that each of us had that the other would see us from very deep within.

Swinging back and forth in continuous and complementary imbalances of unease.

A perfect day, winter sun, almost not cold. Everything very green. The freezing damp house. The lovely garden. The line of leafless poplars, the naked little hill of acacias. The wisteria, almost completely yellow. The two remaining hens have begun clucking now, but they aren't yet laying eggs. In the garden, the cabbages are starting to form heads, the Red Russian kale is at its best, and I gather a full bag every day. I eat it with rice, sautéed with pasta, boiled. I don't like it raw in a salad, it feels too hard. The common kale isn't quite ready yet, although a few leaves can come off now.

The broad beans are useless. And of the peas there is almost nothing left. I harvested some carrots that were thick as a broomstick and quite long. It hasn't frozen yet, and the large Chinese tomato plant is still standing and fruiting. It's incredible. Despite the cold and the rain, there are about six or seven ripe tomatoes and about ten or twelve green ones left to ripen. The chard is big and bushy and I could, if I wanted to, harvest it once in the afternoon and again the next morning.

The soil has aired out enough now, and I've transplanted the cabbages and kales from the second batch to the large bed, along with the peas and cut-leaf mustard. I raked a little again and redid the bed that the pigs had destroyed. I also built another little bed on one side, where the green beans had been.

I haven't seen my neighbour since the night of the storm. Sometimes I hear the truck coming and going, but always at night, late. There's no longer as much of a pig smell as before.

Luiso wraps the taps with burlap, covers them with an upside-down twenty-litre bucket. He says it's going to freeze tonight, and that we need to prepare. At midnight, I wake up freezing, add another blanket, throw my thick jacket over the foot of the bed. I feed a couple more logs into the woodstove.

The sun comes up, and there's a two-centimetre layer of ice on the cows' water troughs. Luiso comes early and chips away at them, breaking them up with a stick. Little ice chips crunch under the soles of my boots as I walk on the stiff grass. With each breath, the ice-cold air like a punch to my lungs, my lips numb, unfeeling, quivering but as if they belonged to someone else.

A continuous pain in my shoulders from going around all day hunching them inward, retracting them to conceal my chest from the cold, like chickens, like hens, like birds, concentrated on themselves, condensed inwards, on their dry little twig.

There are no longer any traces of summer in the garden. The frost destroyed everything. I've taken the zinnias, the marigolds, the tomatoes, the green beans, I've taken the last green squash. They all dried out immediately, after the frost. With the rain, they turned into rotting fibres, damp and grey.

I go around dirty all day, with the smell of smoke in my clothes, in my hair, on my sooty skin, with mud under my nails. My body covered by several layers of cloth. My skin covered. Dog smell stuck in my hair. My clothes that I don't change. Filth as a way of keeping warm. The rhythm of winter acting on my body.

I wake up with a stuffy nose. Headache, congestion, a kink in my neck. Lethargy, the desire to do nothing, the lowest-grade fever. I make myself coffee with milk, add wood to the stove, sit down to read.

Soon I met his mother and sister. We started having Sunday lunch together. At first Ciro would cook, alternating fresh ravioli with baked chicken with salads. Gradually I took over the menu and the kitchen. I met his little nephew. At the first of those lunches, he couldn't have been more than two and a half, three. We were fast friends. We drew with crayons on big sheets of brown paper. We unfurled them on the ground and made tracks for toy cars, putting in trees and houses on the side of the road. With boxes from tea and medicines we built ramps, bridges, buildings. We stuck them on with masking tape, with a box cutter I made doors, windows, lofts, attics.

Then, later on, the age of fart jokes, burping contests, and competitions of who'd eaten the most disgusting food in the whole wide world:

One time I ate a dinosaur's snot!

Well I've had hippopotamus poop!

I ate dog brain!

I ate spider tongue!

Luminous Sundays in that high-perched home, the apartment filled with sun. Sun coming in everywhere, bathing in white light the floorboards, the pale wooden table, the plants climbing up along the window.

Ciro's father had gone back to live in his village a long time before. He went to Buenos Aires very occasionally, every two or three months. When he was visiting, we had dinner with him on Saturdays. Sometimes at Ciro's house, and sometimes he'd take us out to a restaurant he liked.

The day the phone rang, and Ciro learned his grandmother had died. I didn't think he should travel alone, by bus, so I offered to take him. It was a long trip, six or seven hours behind the wheel. We got there as the town was starting to wake up from its siesta. A flat, low town, streets with few trees, not very different from Cabrera, but more humid, hotter, with more of a river and summer smell.

The funeral home was on the square. Right away Ciro's dad came out to receive us.

'This is my son's gay boyfriend,' he said as he introduced me to all their relatives.

He only skipped a couple of ancient aunts and a distant cousin who had been in the military and was retired now.

In a story about orphans, the unremitting impulse to have them encounter a house, have them find shelter.

Tired of eating chard, I give Luiso a full bag and take another into the town to see if anybody wants it. I leave it with Anselmo so that he can give it to whomever he pleases.

I also offer him kale.

What is that? Anselmo asks me as if it stinks or is contagious, keeping a certain distance as he examines the bag with the freshly cut leaves.

I explain it to him.

Kale, kale, he repeats. But what does it taste like?

It's kind of halfway between chard and cabbage, I guess. It's fashionable now, people say it's a superfood.

Anselmo nods.

I don't think anybody around here'll want it, he says.

Do you want me to leave you a little so you can try it? I offer.

To tell you the truth I don't eat much of that kind of

stuff, so you'd better just take it with you, but thank you, though, says Anselmo.

I walk home slowly, with the bag of kale hanging from my fingers. It's voluminous, but light. From far away I see a truck pulling out very slowly, fully loaded, all the way to the top, from the yard where the brick kilns operate. It turns to head in the direction of Lobos and appears to be leaning a little to one side. It stops. A cough of black smoke erupts from its exhaust pipe. Then, as if stuttering, it starts again. It moves slowly over the mud but doesn't slip. It splashes water from the puddles along its path.

The sky is leaden, and at any moment, it could start pouring rain again, so instead of going around the back way, I stay on the main road. When I pass in front of the yard with the ovens, I am surprised to see that everything is calm, quiet. There is no tractor going around in the yard, nor cutters making adobe, nor piles drying, nor any smoke anywhere. I can see the two excavator shovels parked in the background, one of them has its cabin covered in black tarps. Only the manager remains, with a squeegee he takes from one of the puddles that have formed on one of the fields. I recognize him from afar, he was one of the people who helped me move. I go up to say hello.

What's going on? I ask, gesturing at the pits, the mountains of dirt, the pile of broken and discarded bricks, the orange surface of the ground, made up of the powder of thousands and thousands of bricks over the years.

Nothing, he says and takes off his cap in greeting, leaning both his arms against the handle of the squeegee. That was the last batch, he says and indicates the road going to Lobos.

You're not going to do it anymore? I ask. You're closing?

The season is over. With the humidity like this, the adobe doesn't air out anymore. Until the weather gets better, there's nothing that can be done.

Nothing?

He shakes his head.

Until end of August, start of September, depending on the year, he says. It's always been this way, and this is the way it'll always be. In the winter, we rest.

Have you been doing this for a long time? I ask.

My family's made bricks for years. My grandfather's grandfather was already making bricks. It's easy here, there's more than enough soil for the bricks. Whenever we run out, we just move over.

I nod.

I built a house for myself once, I tell him.

The man looks at me. He smiles.

Me too, he says.

Do you still live there? I ask him.

Yes, says the man. I still live there, with my wife and our kids. It's that way, he said and pointed toward the town. Over there.

In Zapiola?

No, it's on past Zapiola.

Then I offer him a little kale, but like Anselmo, he says no, but thank you.

For a few months we looked at apartments. The idea was to rent out Ciro's place, add that to what my rent had been, and move in together somewhere bigger. But we couldn't find our perfect place, or nothing that fell in our price range that we liked. The routine of every afternoon of looking at the ads on ZonaProp and peering into the intimacy of the still-warm dead, or families newly separated, flash-lit photos of stains on the walls, dark hallways, patios that weren't patios, quotidian sadness, laundry rooms full of dirty clothes, basins lined with sediment, stagnant water.

Ultimately, it was his idea: why not build up, onto his own place, adding a room, a desk and a bathroom to what until then had been an unusable terrace. At some point, soon after Ciro had bought his apartment, an architect had told him such a project would be possible and had even drawn up a few quick plans, saying he could even build a very large balcony, with a pergola, a flowerbed, a mini vegetable garden, lots of plants.

We arranged the largest pieces of furniture in a corner that seemed safe. We packed up his library in black bags so the dust wouldn't get into his books, and so they wouldn't be splattered by fresh cement or paint. Ciro, with his cat and all his plants, moved into my apartment for the duration of the renovations. It was almost four months of living in a kind of jungle with lots of duplicate furniture. During that time, a roof caved in, a pipe burst, the house flooded, the builders' estimate tripled, we went into debt, we struggled with the workers day after day, struggled with the costs of the materials, the paint, the openings, the hardware.

To keep costs down, we spent weekends and many afternoons sanding doors, painting walls, putting in sealants, Cetol wood finishes, antirust paint, stripping gel, varnish, layer upon layer. We searched for the best prices, learned a lot about materials and hardware, flooring and insulation. Building a staircase. Electrical installations and everything about the water pipes.

The new tank, the bars for the windows, the railing, the big four-leaf door that led from the bedroom to the terrace, the paint samples, the samples of sockets and light switches, the closet doors and its interiors, the impossible expense of electrical appliances, afternoons hanging around lighting stores, going back and forth between four or five lamps, considering again and again the little label where the prices hung, adding, subtracting. Checking the expiration date of the credit card. Going to the bank to exchange more dollars for pesos.

New words that began to fill our conversations: cremone bolts, plastering trowels, static ropes, wet sanders, waterproofing paste, concrete bonding.

We were tired, and happy, and at every moment we were scared that something would explode, that the tiles would fall off, that the builders would run away with the money, that the room would be too small or too large, that what was happening for us wasn't real.

Little by little, they started putting up walls: brick by brick. Something solid was growing, something stable, big: a house, our house.

We had built a house.

We'd built a shelter, and we'd shut ourselves inside it, to live out all our naps and late nights.
All the kisses, the hugs, the jokes, the endless talks.
All the moments when we would look for each other when we came out of the shower, or right when we woke up, or quickly before dinner, or slowly, both of us tired, when returning from a trip.

The dawn sun licking our sleeping bodies. Ciro's smile, his joy. His breath on his pillow.

Our house, a little fortress where you could sleep with the windows open, three stories above the rest of the world.

Opening your eyes and seeing only sky, the immensity of the immense sky that is empty, vast, and wonderful.

It's been raining every day for twenty days now. It is the season of drizzle, and heavy, intermittent showers. The road is a big mess of mud, maybe a single firm track that gets lost and disappears among the pools, the mudflats, the puddles. Cold, cloudy.

It's rained so much that there is water everywhere, mud. Puddled, stagnant water. The floor tiles inside the house are always damp and ice-cold. As soon as the sun goes down, the grass gets wet, a layer of knee-high fog covers the fields. Damp, cold. All the old people in the town fear getting sick.

When I light the woodstove, the damp condenses, and the walls become wet on the inside, dripping water. Not to lose heat, I close doors, leaving my desk and the kitchen to fend for themselves.

Two doves, very still on their branch, as water falls on them. It falls and falls. Each drop draws a circle that expands in the puddle at the foot of the tree. And each new drop interrupts the expansion of the old circle and traces a new one. This, times a thousand, simultaneously, all the time.

Darkness descends over the garden. It was a short, winter day. At no point did the sun shine. The transparent black sky defines the opaque darkness of the earth.

Dawn. A dense white fog envelops everything. The grass is drenched. The dew hangs onto the edges of the long leaves, arched by the weight of the drops. The dew turns the deep green of the grass almost blue, almost grey, almost silver. The smoke from the chimney floats down to the ground, stagnates, its smell filling the whole yard, the veranda, the garden. My steps are marked in the grass with traces of dense, black mud. Little by little, the sun turns the fog pink. It's very cold. A damp cold that creeps into your bones.

The road is covered in mud. Impassable. The neighbour's tractor can be heard, but not the pigs any longer. A man walks by on the road. He's wearing rubber boots, a beret, and several layers of sweaters. He doesn't have a jacket on. I look to see if he's my neighbour, but no, he's not. Or at least he doesn't look like him.

It rains all the time. Without breaks. You can't do anything. Whole days when the rain is a constant murmur. It numbs. Eating, going out, adding wood to the stove, everything is an effort. A fight. Getting dirty. Getting wet. If I could, I'd do nothing but sleep all day long.

A little house, in the middle of the grassland. Cramped, with little windows, dark inside. Soup. Steam escaping pots on a winter morning. When the lid of the saucepan starts to rattle, I lower the heat.

Winters in Cabrera are different. Dusty and very dry, with a different palette: luminous greys, beige, browns, less saturated colours. The smell of extreme cold. A smell of ozone mixed with the smells of guadal and dust clouds. The smell of wind. Dust always floating, or settling so slowly your eyes can't quite catch it. Its smell stays in your hair, it sticks to your skin, it accumulates in the bowls of your ears, your lips get chapped, your skin cracks, dry earth in your nose, in the corners of your eyes. Here in Zapiola, on the other hand, the smell is one of damp, of mud, of stagnant water, of rotten things, of everything being wet all the time.

Things grow mouldy in the closet. Steely grey, mineral green fungal weals. Thousands of little black fungal dots. Verdigris sprouts on the leather backs of the chairs, and on my jacket, and on my raincoat that hangs on the coat rack.

Last night it rained again all night, and I don't know how much, because the rain gauge reads up to one hundred and twenty millimetres, but I haven't gone out to empty it for several days, and so it's overflowing. Water everywhere. Flooded patio, flooded garden, the alley of poplars is underwater, water in the fields, the main road is flooded. You can't use the bathroom because the cesspool is overflowing, and water comes gushing out the drain. Now wind, cold. The wind has blown the storm away, but it's still cloudy. Grey day. The house surrounded by water.

Stagnant floodwater. In the middle of the field, a corridor between two pools that reflect it. The train embankment.

Some mornings Luiso doesn't even come anymore.

Whole days when I don't see the sky, just low, heavy grey clouds. I miss the clean, blue, transparent air. I go to feed the chickens. They get excited when they see me, they cluck, they come up to the door. I throw them two handfuls of cracked corn and the remains of the organic garbage. Leek caps, carrot leaves, potato peelings. The chickens are dirty, damp, their stuck-together feathers reveal the yellow skin below and make them look like little vultures from a domestic garbage dump, emaciated and malnourished. All the same, they peck in the mud, splash in the puddles with pleasure, they splash and run away with a leaf in their beak, thrilled, as if they're doing something forbidden, as if the leaf were a treasure, and they were pulling off some kind of heist.

You have to make mention of some things because if you don't, they don't exist; others have to be passed over in silence, so that they aren't there. Clouds need to be noted. The sky. All the birds, each of the grasses. Sometimes I conduct an experiment: I walk and try to list everything I see. The leaves of a bush I don't know the name of, a fence post, a rod, the tracks left in the mud by the tractors this morning.

What has to be kept quiet, for instance, is mysteries. Stick to naming things. Look at them from the outside only. What's inside can't be seen. What's inside should not be spoken of.

It is bizarre to be someone, to be inside oneself and with oneself at every moment, with oneself at every rotten turn. And calculating how much others can see, what they assume, what you allow them to know. Being inside and not saying it. Silence. Silence.

One day, when we had moved into the new house, Ciro sent me that Wojnarowicz photograph on WhatsApp, in black and white, the one of the buffaloes falling off the cliff.

It's the saddest photo I've ever seen in my life, he said. And it's the one I like the most.

The long dark hallway, the neighbour's Chinese jasmine that climbed over the dividing wall and filled the cool nights with its fragrance. The narrow staircase, the succulents on the landing; the giant concrete Playmobil-style figure I gave Ciro one Christmas and that performed the function of garden gnome there among the plants. The two ficuses, the white sheet metal door, slightly pitted toward the bottom. The smoothed concrete floor. The enormous windows. A miniature world made out of plants, recycled tiles from the sixties, a magnetic steel band for hanging knives, the countertop that was also made of concrete, the green trash can up against the wall, and the wall that would always get dirty, and the old refrigerator. I was in charge of cooking, Ciro would wash the dishes. Hardwood furniture; dolls and children's toys on his bookshelves, snapshots and portraits on mine; Ciro's study beneath the staircase that went up to the third floor – the new part – the large divided-light window; the enormous closet, his side of the closet, mine; my drawers suddenly empty; the central unit we shared to hang shirts, coats; his drawers, folding the dry clothes, separating the t-shirts and arranging them on his shelves or on mine; the drawer where we kept the lubricant, the condoms; our bed; the iPad on his side, resting on the floor; my chair that served as a nightstand, covered in books and a lamp that Ciro had given me; the little window right above the headboard, on his side of the bed, which as soon as we had finished the renovation he regretted having made, taking an unwavering hatred to it; my desk, facing the white wall so that I wouldn't get distracted, the postcards stuck to the wall with masking tape, the pile of paper to recycle and print on both sides; the huge French doors, with the old peeling white paint that we'd decided not to sand because we liked it the way it was; the terrace and its brick-coloured tiles, its iron railings; the light on the neighbours' metal water tanks; the crowns of the trees out there, along the sidewalks, above the roofs of the other homes; all our flowerpots: grasses growing almost wild, foxtails, fountaingrasses, New Zealand flax, shrubs and seasonal flowers, the seedlings we went to look for at the Agronomía nursery every spring, four or five jasmines; the boxes where we planted sage, thyme, oregano, where in spring I would plant arugula and lettuce and mizuna, where one summer we tried to grow tomatoes and they died suddenly one day, scorched by the midday sun; the low chairs where we sat to watch the sunset; the tap where we plugged in the hose to water the plants – morning and afternoon in summer, every three or four days in winter; the nights sleeping with the window open, looking at the stars, January in Buenos Aires, Ciro's raspy breathing, which didn't rise to snoring; the cool breeze, the empty city, a certain randomness of the traffic lights and not much traffic on the avenue and that strange occasion, in the early morning, when the city was, for three full minutes, suspended in a perfect silence.

All that we built together
with so much care, with so much love.

Naming everything that doesn't belong to me now.
Naming all the years when there were two of us.

Time passes easily in movies, in novels. Only important actions are narrated, the ones that advance the plot. The rest – the doubts, the boredom, the long days where nothing changes, the stagnant sadness – vanishes into ellipses, clean cuts, quick summaries.

A romantic comedy. Boy meets girl. Or boy meets

boy. Or girl meets girl. Neither the gender nor the orientation matters, toward the middle the protagonists separate, cue the little leitmotif, a calendar superimposed on the screen, and the sheets with the months fly off quickly, carried away by the wind. The main character strolling along the banks of a river, the protagonist working at a desk, the song still playing: it's summer, it's fall. Character A runs over dry leaves. Suddenly it's winter, and Character B adjusts their scarf as they walk through a snowstorm. Spring again, A leaves their house, buys a bouquet of flowers. The ditty resumes, summer, an easy solution for the screenwriters who no longer have to worry about how to handle time.

What do sad people in movies do with all the hours in a day? What do they do when the little ditty isn't playing?

It is as though during mourning there cannot be narrative.

Yesterday, as soon as the drizzle had begun to subside, I put on my rubber boots and trudged into town. It was late, I took a flashlight in case it got dark while I was on my way back. At the entrance to town, before I reached the square, in the area that marks the limits of the reach of the antennae and my cell got reception again, I texted Ciro:

Can I call?

What's wrong?

Nothing I just need to ask you something

Ok. But I can't talk long. I'm working.

Are we in the part with the leitmotif? I asked him as soon as he picked up. Is this the time we have to spend apart so that each of us faces our darkness, our individual fears, and then, at a distance, understands our love is true and that we have to end up together? Is this the time of being apart and descending into hell that we have to take in order to heal our wounds, transform ourselves and then choose each other again from a healthier, brighter place, a new place?

Ciro took a minute to respond.

Then he said, No. I don't think so.

But Ciro, we built a home together.

You want to start this all over again? Ciro said.

I didn't know what to answer.

Our story is over, Ciro said then. I'm in a different place now. Don't wait on me. I don't want to get back together with you. I don't think I'll want to later on.

I'd been just talking to myself for so long that I'd forgotten the sound of his voice.

JULY

It didn't rain at all today. A miracle. Clear sky. At four-thirty the sun starts to go down, the light grows gold, orange, amber. Shadows elongate. At half past five it's almost night. I take advantage of the last light of day to harvest a little chard, some common kale leaves, and a bit of arugula. So much mud on the road it's impassable. Puddled water. Flooded fields, flooded roads. A stork walks, stride slow, head down, beak casting about in the water. It's very cold. The stalks of the cabbage lean to one side in the mud. I shore them up with soil, working with the hoe, maybe they'll manage to survive. Little by little their heads have been gaining weight, the leaves wrapping around themselves, tightening.

Days made up of small discomforts, uncertainties, as though I'm floating without going anywhere. Little changes in my mood. Tiredness. Unpleasantness. Looking. Complaints. Everything very light, very superficial. Everything just for a little while. Days without consistency, without being able to get going. Without doing anything much. Maybe it is just tiredness, or longing, or boredom in the face of so much rain, so much water.

I go through old folders, dig around in my files, first drafts, efforts, stories left unfinished. I read the first pages, scroll down. I don't remember vast tracts of what I wrote. I don't understand what I was trying to achieve, what I wanted.

I can't read myself.

Not yet, I mean.

Like in a garden, all things take time, grow little by little, and at any moment, everything may go awry, ants may come, an infestation, or the wind, hail may fall, plants may go to seed, come to nothing, not fruit, be in vain.

It is always more pleasant not to write. All your energy stays in the service of pleasure: there is no risk, there is no motion, there is harmony.

Writing requires chaos, uncertainty, turmoil. It's something that grows, like the chard at the top: messy and up. It requires a certain fortitude and also strength and not really knowing where to direct that strength.

It's a little like building a house without a plan: digging, laying a solid foundation, trying for a structure that will give meaning and shape, building, little by little, walls, word after word, brick after brick, and when it's not working, tearing everything down, demolishing, starting all over. Until finally making it to the point of thick plaster, fine plaster, little details, lighting certain corners, installing a few door handles, key holes to peek through. And even still, there is always something in the wrong set square, always something that will rupture, that will burst.

How to write now? How to write in the wake of? Is it possible to keep writing the way I did before? I hesitate. I take a lot of notes. I go all out on notes I don't even end up using. I add word after word as though each weighed a thousand kilos, as though each word entailed an enormous physical effort. Word by word, brick by brick. With every one I'm afraid that the whole structure will come tumbling down, that the house will fall apart, that it cannot withstand the weight of the roof. With every one I'm afraid of making a mistake, not being up to par, making a fool of myself, of an incoming gale that will destroy me completely.

And so I sit here, having let out the chickens, and I watch the clouds over the still field, feeling the cold over my body.

Crystalline sound in the frozen night. Layer of fog. A dog in a distant scrimmage. The town in the dark. Everyone inside their house, protecting themselves from sub-zero temperatures.

The sensation of lives laid to waste.

The cruelty of the countryside. The not knowing anymore what I'm doing here, the why, if I'm not even writing, if it's not even passing, if I'm not even forgetting. Life is now an image that is blurring, losing its shape day by day. The rusticity, the hassles, the cold the countryside confronts you with, the profundity of the black of the sky. There's nothing more to be done. Turn on the stove. Read. Wait for winter to ease its grip.

Learning the slow time of growing things. Of winter, which slows things down.

The oakleaf lettuce seems to like the cold, it's grown quite strong and healthy, despite the rain, despite the frost. The calendulas and the larkspur vegetate there, not progressing but also apparently not dying. The mustard came up immediately and has already put out its second set of leaves. The little sun there is hits directly through the naked poplars, lighting them up and bringing out in them green gleams.

The only Brussels sprout seedlings that I'd managed to make sprout rotted almost without growing at all. One of the common cabbages went to rot, one day it was drowned in a tide of grey aphids, so stuck to the leaves they almost looked like moss. I tried to remove them, but they had already got inside, so I pulled it out completely and threw it into the henhouse.

The segments of hydrangea and sage that I'd placed in pots to see if they'd take have completely frozen. I should have covered them.

There's still a lot of kale, a lot of chard. The first leeks, not too thick yet: like a little finger, but that's enough. I tear off a few, just the necessary ones, and let the others keep adding rings.

What's done nothing at all is the beets. At this point I'm tired, I'm not going to keep planting radishes.

Yesterday, while working in the garden, I saw the neighbour over the fence, on the other side of the road. He was leaning against the tin wall of his shed, looking at his hands with his head down, counting something on his fingers. One. Two. Three. Four. There he remained, with his four fingers out. Then he closed his hand and started counting again. Index, middle, ring, little finger, and then he started again. He did that for a long time. He seemed calm. Not worried or anything, just calm. A dog was sleeping by his side. At one point I thought the neighbour was going to glance in the direction of my garden, and I raised my arm to greet him, but in the end, he didn't move. The dog pricked his ears a little and just kept sleeping. I forgot to tell Luiso that this morning.

One of the broccoli plants looks like it's trying to flower. Strange with this cold. The cauliflower still hasn't given any indication of life.

The grass is very green. All the naked branches on the trees.

How to write amid the wreckage, in the mud and the puddles, collecting, here and there, the wet remains of what was once a day-to-day, of what was once a home?

How to write a story amid the wreckage of a history?

Snapped leaves, worn-down shoes, coffee pots stained with mud, broken plates, shattered plates, pieces of glasses, fragments of conversations, footsteps on the stairs, smells, sometimes smells that appear to me in dreams, or suddenly, like a sharp pain, an electric spark.

'When you are in the middle of a story it isn't a story at all, but only a confusion; a dark roaring, a blindness, a wreckage of shattered glass and splintered wood…. It's only afterwards that it becomes anything like a story at all,' writes Margaret Atwood.

The major energy that writing requires is that of ordering, that of telling the story, that of giving it an order and a structure, that of establishing its meaning.

It's hard to resist the temptation of an ordered world.

That sensation of control narration gives: control over the past, control over the story, control over what is to come, over what might or might not end up happening.

Words' speed seduces you by making you believe you'll be able to put the world in order by banging on your keyboard. Structuring, ordering, narrating perfect, harmonious, safe worlds, and the illusion that the world is becoming perfect, harmonious, safe. That, like in the story, things, all these things, also mean something.

Telling ourselves that story in order to keep going. Making sure the sketch that gets drawn is, at least, pleasing to the eye.

At the end of the day, we're merely characters in search of a plot that would lend meaning to our story, trying to identify the narrative we're in, making sure, right here and now, that the ending is going to be happy, or at least, good, or at least, worthy.

It's soothing to feel life has a shape.

Not asking of writing what writing cannot possibly give.

Many years ago, in my late twenties, at a routine check-up, my doctor told me that if my blood pressure continued at its current levels, we'd have to increase the dosage of my medication, add a diuretic, or take action.
It's a lot for your age, he said.

At that time I was still living in Córdoba, teaching classes at a university, hosting workshops, I'd published a couple of books. I'd had high blood pressure since the age of eighteen: the pressure that the body puts on itself. How the body itself presses inward – curls in on itself, closes – and crushes/contracts arteries and veins.

The causes of the elevation weren't entirely clear. Maybe salt consumption, and my sedentary lifestyle, yes, but maybe also the pressure to *be* that I was putting on myself. I had already left, but I felt that I still wasn't able to *be*. At that time I was taking Amlodipine, the same dose and the same medication as my grandfather – then an old man of seventy-some years. Every time I went to Cabrera and forgot my pills, I would ask him to give me some of his.

At that same appointment, the doctor recommended exercise – which I was doing barely any of – or meditation, or 'some type of work therapy'.

Work therapy? I asked.

Something you do with your hands, said the doctor. Carpentry, knitting, painting, something that you like and that helps you slow down your thoughts.

Monyu, one of my friends, was a ceramicist, and I decided to take classes with her. Every Thursday afternoon I would go to her workshop, and Monyu would have me knead clay, mix glazes, and make pinch pots. Then, when a certain amount of time had passed, she sat me down in front of a wheel.

The process of wheel-throwing is simple: with pressure and water, an amorphous mass of clay – well-kneaded, to ensure that no bubbles or air chambers remain inside – is stuck onto a rotating surface, then a motor is turned on, the amorphous mass begins to rotate and, with a little more water, out of the effort of your hands, that mass starts to take on a shape and become something useful, recognizable, rewarding.

The first thing to do is make sure it's lined up. This is called 'centring,' and it is essential if you want the process to give a decent result. Lining up, centring, with the strength – and you need quite a bit of strength – of your palms and the fingers of both your hands, pushing the clay inward, pushing it in on itself so that it absorbs and loses whatever asymmetry it may possess and – thanks to centripetal force – finds a harmonious balance that allows it to turn and turn in peace.

To achieve this, part of it is knack – the posture, the exact and precise forces you have to apply with your hip, with your back, resting your elbows on your knees, what you do with your hands, what you do with your fingers – and another part is logic: giving a centre to what is amorphous, ensuring its axis coincides with the axis on which the surface of the wheel is rotating.

The pleasure, not even of making a bowl, but of taming a piece of clay, of making it be centred on a wheel. The rest can be done, with greater or lesser skill, only if that centring is successful. After centring, it's just a matter of knowing how to move your hands, of maintaining the right speed: bowls, plates, cups, vases with straight sides, vases with curving sides. They all start from the same place: a centred piece, a harmony that rotates in harmony with an axis.

Centring, balancing, smoothing out, harmonizing. The pleasure of giving a shape to something that had no shape before. The beauty of a fresh bowl in your hands. The pleasure of fire burning it and turning it into something solid, something that will last.

On a wheel, beauty is applying force, energy, it is mastering that which is different and guiding it into a familiar, recognizable body. It is that from different kinds of surfaces, my hands apply a powerful limit, in order to always caress the same thing.

When you write a story, sometimes, something similar occurs: taming the mass of words, facts, ideas, removing the particularities from your imagination, your life, just so as to already have in mind an image of what is good, of what a good story is, of what an admirable story is, of what a beautiful story is.

Like a bowl, like a plate, like hundreds, like thousands of bowls and plates, always identical to one another.

At first, I wanted everything in the garden to be perfect. I drew, I made sketches and plans, I settled the seedlings, arranged the beds, fretted over everything. Little by little, the infestations, the weeds started getting the better of me, and the garden began to just be how it was, untidy and all mixed up. To be whatever way it was managing to be. Or, sometimes, not to be any way at all.

There is a pleasure in shaping, in controlling the shape of things, that is offered by ceramics, and that I used to find in writing, and that gardening doesn't give. The garden requires you to yield: to set it up and then let luck and climate have their way with it, polish it, mould it.

The cold ruins some things, while others it helps. The same thing happens with rain, drizzle, mud, soil that is dark and sticky and dense.

In ceramics, harmony is achieved through skill and by applying force. Beauty involves setting limits, using your muscles, a certain violence, a certain expenditure of energy.

In the garden, there is always something being born, and there is always something dying. If there is any harmony, it is through sheer coincidence, and it lasts only a moment.

I used to think that stories needed to be treated like clay. Now I wonder if you could write the way you make a garden.

A whole week without rain. It's cold and cloudy. Everything is still covered in mud, and in the fields the water isn't draining, but it hasn't rained again.

It's frozen a few times over the past few days, though it never gets as cold as I remember the winters being back in Córdoba. Never impenetrable layers of ice on the tanks, never pipes bursting or lines of frozen white drops extending from a tap someone forgot to turn off.

Luiso says it's because there's so much humidity here, that's why it never gets that cold. The cabbages develop a shiny frosting on the edges of their leaves, on the veins; beyond that, nothing. The chard gets a bit droopy, but just for a couple of days. If I cut off the damaged leaves at once I can eat them with no issues. Kale, carrots, leeks – it's like they can't feel the cold. Every night I cover up the lettuce with some cloth.

Yesterday there was no rice left, no more pasta, not much yerba mate, it had been four days since I'd last eaten meat, just chard, kale, carrots, and whatever else there was in the garden. I grabbed my backpack, put on my jacket and boots and walked through the mud to the big road. A pool of seven or eight hundred metres. Water all the way across, from fence to fence. A leaden sky. My cheeks taut, eyes and nose watering form the cold. I went out right as a row of trucks passed by, heading toward Lobos, away from the little town. You could tell the base of the road was still solid, because they moved slowly, but without sliding or spinning their tyres. Not one got stuck. The water reached over their fenders. But they made their way, sending out big fans of brownish water on either side. It looked like a parade. From one of the trucks, a little boy in a white coat waved to me. They must have been taking him to school.

The back road, a little higher up, was covered in puddles, but it wasn't flooded. You could walk on it easily.

Lots of different kinds of ducks. I counted five or six species. I'd like to know a little more, to be able to identify them.

In the final stretch, after the rectangle of forest, just before reaching the village, a lagoon of a hundred or a hundred and fifty metres across. I was trying to decide if I should climb over into the field to bypass it or if my boots would be high enough to wade through it when I saw a pickup approaching from the direction of the marsh. The driver pulled up next to me and waved to me to get in. I clambered into the bed, since my boots were covered in mud, and if I sat up front I'd foul up his whole floor. Besides, up front, in the passenger's seat, there was a dog.

We started the crossing, and in the middle of the lagoon the Rastrojero lost its traction and started to lurch. I thought we were going to get stuck, but the driver expertly steered the wheel, the engine wheezed in the water, the Rastrojero hacked, the whole chassis shook, and we managed to get through unscathed.

I was left at the entrance to the village, almost right where the lagoon ended, and they headed on, toward the square. The driver said goodbye to me by honking his horn, and the dog stuck his head out the window to watch me with his tongue hanging out.

Lots of silence in Zapiola. Cloudy sky, calm morning. All I could hear all around me was the cry of the chimangos, the sound of my boots as they splatted through the mud. I stopped by the butcher's and then went to Anselmo's.

How did you get here? On foot? he asked as he rubbed his hands in front of the screen of the stove, glued to the tank.

I told him about the giant puddle, about the Rastrojero.

Must have been Cupri, he's the only one with a Rastrojero. Did he have a dog with him up front?

I said he did.

There you go. That was Cupri, Anselmo said with a nod.

I asked him for cheese, crackers, yerba mate, and some pasta.

Winters are tough around here, he said, and he turned to gather my things from his shelves.

Later, as I was heading home, in the middle of the field that separates the town's two centres, I ran into a man who was coming from the direction of the chapel. He was an older man, I'd never seen him before. His mouth was sunken and tight, as though he had forgotten his false teeth somewhere. He was wearing a knee-length green jacket. He was bent over, but walking with determination toward the train station.

Clutched to his chest was a shoebox wrapped in a nylon bag. He held it to his body as though someone, at any moment, might snatch it away from him.

I said hello, but he didn't so much as look at me. He seemed alarmed, his eyes alert, his brow furrowed. I turned around.

Are you all right, sir? Do you need any help? I asked him.

Without even slowing, the old man quickly raised an arm, as though to tell me to go fuck myself, and continued on his way.

On his feet he was wearing a pair of those slippers grandpas wear, felt or something similar to felt. They didn't have so much as a splotch on them, and he walked in them at full speed, without faltering, along over the mud.

Yesterday I found another chicken, the third, dead in the coop. She was near the fence, lying on the ground with a muff of feathers scattered around her on the wet earth.

On her back there was a large wound, a tear that went down to the bone. There was blood, and her yellow hide was visible, her flesh. Her head flopped to one side. Her eye was open, staring, her pupil reflecting the sky and the branches of the eucalyptus tree.

The other chicken – the only one left – was inside. She immediately ran to eat when I threw some corn to her. She didn't seem injured or to have lost feathers. She was calm. I checked the woven wire, the door. I couldn't find any gaps anywhere or anything out of the ordinary. I'd been at home all afternoon and hadn't heard a single sound.

I told Luiso in the morning.

It couldn't have been a dog, I told him. And I doubt it was a weasel at that hour, in broad daylight. Maybe it was a fox? The wire was intact, I don't know how it could have got in.

It was a caracara, Luiso said. It has to have been a caracara. Was her back bitten?

I said yes.

You see, it was a caracara. They must be running out of food. Was your chicken laying yet?

No, neither one of them. They haven't started.

Luiso sighed, shook his head.

You didn't get a very good deal on those chickens, he said.

I look out at the countryside and am overcome by anxiety.

It has to do with wondering what it means. What does countryside mean? The horizon, the grassland, the clouds casting shadows over the field.

Nothing. They mean nothing. They just are.

It's like standing in front of a cathedral, or something else immense.

Is it like standing before God?

It's simply contemplating.

There's no need for contemplation to lead to any conclusion. Just contemplate. Don't analyse. Don't overthink.

The shape of a puddle in the mud means nothing. It just is.

Things are.

Look at them.

Don't put them in order. Don't organize them into stories. Don't look for a cause, a reason for their being, an end. Don't organize them. Don't give them meaning.

'The real question isn't, what does this mean? But rather, what is it?' I remember hearing Anish Kapoor saying that, or something like it, in an interview some years ago.

If I were to stop writing, what would happen?
If I were to stop writing, who would I be?

What I like about the garden is that you don't have to think. All you have to do is do things. You thrust in the shovel, loosen the soil, rake, weed, sow, get covered in mud, prune, come, go. Do, do, do. The body gets tired. The mind goes blank.

Writing, on the other hand, is non-stop thinking. Trying to translate everything into words. Trying to get as close as possible to finding names for things. The mind exhausts itself in that impossible precision, feels like it's going to explode.

How to narrate without story? Without order? Without trying to make it make sense?
Simply narrating, not trying to understand as you go.

A story that would be darkness and, only occasionally, flashes of orange light, or red, or white, or yellow.

A story like a succession of fireworks. They begin, they explode, they end. There's no point to it, no meaning. They simply burst into the night, burn with raucous, sizzling beauty, and then there's just smoke, in the end, there's just night.

Fires, but also works.

Explosions to look at, so that people can sense them vibrate in their pupils, feel a dusting of ash or embers on their skin.

Creating fires so that some small part of them, small and also unpredictable, will gleam in someone else's eyes, for just an instant. Impossible to tell whose eyes. Impossible to say what small part.

Silly explosions, illogical, plotless. Do I risk having the reader set aside the book, having them decide it's bad?

That is always the only fear: rejection. By my father, by my family, by my town.

That is the unnarratable pain: Ciro's rejection.

Imprisoned by the need to organize the story, to tell the story well, not to bore, to be entertaining, to create plots and seduce with intrigue, to be more and more original, to tell more and more perfect stories. Out of a fear of rejection, not being able to be free.

'What if a life had no discernible narrative, no coherent main action?' asked James Wood in an article I read the other day. 'Actual lives look nothing much like conventional novels.'

That first night, after the funeral, I offered to spend the night at my grandmother's house so she wouldn't have to spend it alone. I drove us out to the country. The shape of my grandfather's body still moulded into the seat of his truck. The pedals far away, because he was taller; the gear shift worn from feeling the touch of his hand so often; his letters, some receipts, some invoices in the rear window, as if he'd just picked up his mail. One of his notebooks in the door, next to the chamois and the insurance papers.

We took the same route as always: Güero Road, Hanged Man Road, Perdices Road, Juan Pancho's land, Juan Jorge's. My grandmother looked ahead, her hands crossed on her skirt. Silence.

When we got there, on the kitchen counter, we found a gourd filled with dry yerba mate, left there no doubt in the rush of everything. My grandmother said nothing, just emptied the yerba mate into the trash can, washed the gourd out in the sink.

In the bathroom, still, his razors, his toothbrush, his blood pressure pills, his Bakelite combs.

Someone had left a window open, and a layer of dust covered the tiles in the bedroom, I could feel it under my bare feet.

I made tea for my grandma. I asked her if she needed anything, if she was doing okay.

The sheets on my bed were frozen, extremely cold. Months on end, years, without anyone sleeping in that bed.

I tried to read a while but couldn't concentrate. The lines began to blur before my eyes, so I left the book on the nightstand and went to the bathroom.

As I passed by the door of her bedroom, I saw my grandmother lying very still, on her back, looking at the ceiling, the closet, the brown curtains that covered the windows, the same curtains as always, the same curtains as in all those long years.

Do you want me to turn off your light? I asked her.

No, she said. I'm going to read a little while.

I nodded and went back to my bed.

At some point, I heard her get up, open and close drawers, looking for something.

Are you okay? I said loudly enough, without moving.

Yes, yes. Go to sleep, it's late, she responded. Do you need more blankets? Are you okay? Are you cold?

I'm okay. I'll read a little while longer and turn out the light.

Then, in the silence of the calm countryside, I heard her going back to bed, the squeak of the mattress as she got comfortable, the rustling of the sheets. The sound of the knob of the lamp when she turned it off. She turned it once or twice. From my room, I could hear her calm, rhythmic breathing. I knew she wasn't asleep, that she was just lying still, on her side of the bed.

Half an hour, or forty-five minutes, passed before her breathing got rougher. Then, almost immediately, she started to snore.

I stayed as I was for a long time, looking at the ceiling, not wanting to turn out my light and not knowing what to do other than listen to her sleep on the other side of the wall.

'That sadness now, of weeds and thistles no one cuts,' I read in a poem by Osvaldo Aguirre.

I walk into the village to call my grandma because it's her birthday. She's turning ninety-two.

I ask how she's doing.

Last night I went to the buffet with my girlfriends, she tells me. I went with Titi Broilo and Nucha Biglia. There weren't very many people there. We shared a grilled cheese sandwich, the three of us, and we ate the

French fries they give you, and the peanuts, that was my dinner. I got home at about nine-thirty, and I stayed in after that.

I ask after her other girlfriends, why so few of them went out to celebrate.

What can you do, she says. All my closest friends, the girls in my posse, are a mess right now. Olga's got the rheumatism, the arthritis, you have to help her up the stairs, if we call a taxi we've got to get her in and out of it. Tere's lucid but blind. She can see a little bit, she can make out shapes, but you have to go everywhere with her, she can't walk on her own. I've got three weeks on her. We're the same age, her birthday's at the end of the month, and she is blind as a bat. Elvita, from across the street here, who is a saint, who if I don't go to see her she'll call me on the telephone, she walks with a walker now. Ana last month ended up getting put in a home, and she's going to stay there, she won't be getting out of there again. The other day they took her to mass, but the priest told her off, made her sit on the pew and told her not to move. She wants to do it, wants to stand up, sit down, but she can't, her legs are in agony, her heart's weak. The only ones I've got left are Nucha and Titi, and even Titi I have to manoeuvre a little because if I leave her alone she'll get lost.

What's going on with Titi? I ask.

Oh, her head isn't right, says my grandma. If I'm there, she trusts me, and she won't get nervous, and she doesn't get disoriented. If I'm not there, she's lost. From you look nice she'll go to what day is today, she'll say she wants to leave, say she has to go see her brother. Her brother died ten years ago, you know? Titi's problem is she never really recovered after she hit her head, but she manages okay, I guess. Recently she took down all the masses in her novena, you know, she loves to take down the masses, but you had to be there with her the whole time, tell her: Titi, do this, turn the page here, read this, read that, and like that she'll do it perfectly, but if you let her loose, she's a disaster.

Poor thing, I said.

I mean, what do you expect, said my grandmother. These things happen. They'll happen to me, too, age brings about all these things, although I'm getting along fine, age brings about all these things. So there you go, that's the story of the girls in my posse. I'm losing all my friends. I'm the most *engambará* of all of them, I'm going to have to get some younger girls around, if not I'm not going to be able to get out of the house at all.

I nod, it's a clear, humid day, the wind strikes my face, pirouettes through my hair. I turn so my back is to the wind so it doesn't buzz on the phone.

When did Titi hit her head? I ask her.

Titi? she says. A long time ago. She fell, she was hit by a car on a trip they'd taken with the retirees. Over to Carlos Paz, they'd gone.

Sometimes I wish I could be an abstract painter. Working with paint and pigments as pure matter. Starting from happiness and innocence and going to matter. Only matter. Abstraction. Non-representation. Being able to do that with language: write something without sound, without having to understand, to clarify, something that comes from the body, something that's only letters, only drawing, words and sentences that mean nothing. Not having to think.

Sometimes I'd love not to say anything, just to make up a list of words that would occupy my time. A list of my favourite words:

Lombote

Lonja
Ponchada
Refucilo
Orear
Fajinar
Tupido
Revienta
Pando
Picaflor
Chilcal
Chinela
The verb *achuzar*
The adjective *chuzo*
Chanfleado, although I don't know if *chanfleado* is a word that is used everywhere or only in Cabrera.

Words to look at. That and nothing more.

Sometimes I just want to stay quiet. Not to speak. Not to write. Not to do anything, for a long time.

Words can't tame the body.

No word can tame, can break sorrow. No word can drive it away.

And no word can actually say it – not really.

AUGUST/SEPTEMBER

There's an older gentleman that wants to meet you, Anselmo told me a few days ago, when I went to buy a lightbulb to replace the one that had burned out in the kitchen.

An older gentleman? Who?

Wendel, he says that every time you pass by his place you try to look inside.

I do? Where does he live?

At the top of the road that leaves the town here and runs along the train tracks. That little plot with all the plants in it.

The forest rectangle? I asked.

That's it.

The forest rectangle! I said. It doesn't look like anybody lives in there, I didn't realize.

Wendel lives in there, Anselmo said, nodding. I already told him you're just curious, but that you seem like a good guy. I'll introduce you to him sometime, don't worry about it.

That afternoon, as I was going home, I walked faster than usual along the forest rectangle and tried to make sure I was looking straight ahead, at the road, just in front of me. Most of the trees in the forest had lost almost all their leaves by then, so that the forest was now an interweaving of grey trunks that overlapped and got lost, but even without leaves, from what I could see quickly, out of the corner of my eye, they revealed no human structure anywhere.

Then, when I turned onto the grassy path and looked back at the rectangle from a distance, I thought I saw a wisp of smoke rising against the low clouds, as if someone inside, I imagined, had lit a wood-fired range, or a woodstove.

Winter clear-cuts and reseeds the easy way, writes Annie Dillard. Little by little new shoots begin to appear between puddles and wet earth. The little acacia from the garden and the acacia from the shed produce clusters of buds at the tips of their branches. Soon they'll be yellow flowers. The freshly cut wet grass sticks to the soles of my boots. Gleaming green. The tall grass. Skies without clouds, without limits. Open, unlimited form.

An afternoon that feels like winter, still. Calm, silent, but sunny. A warmer light. I weed the bed of cabbage and lettuce that survived the frost. The mint is starting to sprout. The peas are totally gone now, but there are good leeks and good cabbages and a semi-decent cauli-flower that's beginning to form a head. The onions seem to want to start to fatten. The broad beans, which have spent the whole winter vegetating sort of lost among the weeds, have suddenly taken off, grown almost twenty centimetres, become upright. I think they might be about to bloom.

It's been the wettest winter in years. We are surrounded by water. The fields can no longer absorb another drop and the water does not go down. What can't move rots. There is mud and, everywhere, the smell of carrion, of fermented grass, of decomposing things.

As soon as the sun goes down, the temperature plummets ten degrees.

Today, by chance, when I came out of the shower, I saw my body reflected in the closet mirror. Not only do I now have a swirl of white grey at the tip of my beard, but also the hairs on my chest have turned grey, almost white. Not all, but quite a few, like a tongue of albino hairs, too fine and thinned out, going down over the nipple, on the left side.

Lots of silence at my neighbour's. I haven't heard him for days, I haven't seen him. I don't know what happened to the pigs. Maybe they were removed at some point, while I was in town. There's no smell anymore, and there's no one coming to feed them. I ask Luiso, but he acts like he doesn't know what I mean.

I think they're still here, he says. I think those pigs are still here.

Who's to say, he says.

Yesterday morning, when I'd finished paying at Anselmo's and we were chatting about when the water was going to go down from the fields and if the biggest rains were finally over, the door to the bar opened and a very tall, skinny man entered, a weathered face, the mark of a hat like an invisible ring pressing in on his stiff grey hair. He must have been in his upper sixties, rubber boots, jeans, and a brown sweater covered in pills.

He didn't offer any greeting, didn't say good morning, or hello, or anything.

He looked me up and down.

You're the guy that gardens, too, he said.

I nodded my head. I smiled.

Do you also have a garden? I asked.

This is Wendel, Anselmo introduced us then.

You always peek in on my place, said Wendel. The other day you stopped on the road and turned to look. I saw you.

I burst out laughing and extended my hand, but he didn't move. He stared at me, he didn't smile back.

I'm very sorry, I said as I put my hand in my pocket. I didn't mean to bother you. I was just curious about all those different trees. You can't see anything inside them. I was just always curious, since I got here.

You like trees? he asked me.

I nodded with enthusiasm.

In that case, said Wendel, you can stop skulking around. If you're curious, stop by whenever you want. I'm always at home, all you have to do is open the gate. The dogs are noisy but they won't do anything to you.

That afternoon I was bored and didn't know what to do, so I went to visit him. On the other side of the gate, the road curved. Beyond the cypresses you could only see the naked branching of the poplars growing pressed together tightly. Then, almost immediately, the path opened onto a clearing, and the house appeared: small, with a gable roof, and brick, almost a cabin with divided-light windows and a sheet metal veranda. Right away the dogs came out to tussle and then, behind the dogs, there was Wendel.

Quiet! Come here! he shouted at them, and the dogs stopped barking and came over to sniff my hands.

Wendel was wearing the same brown pilled sweater and the same boots, but now he didn't bother taking off his hat.

See all these trees? I planted all of them myself, said Wendel.

He had created some small paths through the mass of elms and poplars, tidy little trails, the ground covered in layers of dark, damp, rotting leaves. Without saying much, he motioned for me to follow him. From time to time he would show me with a gesture where to be careful with a branch, where to lower my head, where to put my foot to step over a fallen log, when to turn left or right. The countryside around us had completely disappeared. We were in the forest. You could see the sky only if you threw your whole head back. We were surrounded by a tight, deafening silence. The only thing you could hear were the dogs running ahead, sniffing at the bases of logs, raising a paw to piss on them and, panting, turning to look at what we were doing.

Little by little I began to understand that the paths in the forest made up a regular route. Each one led to a small clearing, a little area trussed up with branches where Wendel had been building, over time, some record, a landmark, a place worth walking to, or interrupting a walk to sit at for a while. There were a couple of little cubbyhole shrines, each with a concrete bench in front: one to the Virgin of Lourdes, made out of cement and covered in tiles and broken mirrors, another to Saint Benedict, a miniature wood cabin.

In the centre of a kind of rotunda where three different paths led there was a stone drinking fountain. And a few metres further on, surrounded by some ferns that had been damaged by the freezing cold, there was a replica of the headless Venus de Milo, her shoulders and breasts covered up to the height of the nipples by a layer of very green and shiny moss that was almost phosphorescent among so many dull greys and browns.

Wendel showed it all to me without words. He would pause for just a moment, and with a tilt of his head or a gesture of his hand, he would point out the Virgin, the Venus, Saint Benedict's shrine. I stood there not really knowing what to say. Then Wendel would nod, summon the dogs, and continue walking.

In another area, farther up, deeper within the forest, after three or four bends in the path, from among the trees, there emerged an abstract steel and metal sculpture. A huge polished dazzling circle, embedded among twisted iron. From the centre of the circle, obliquely, rose a piece of rusted beam that pointed upward.

It's a tribute, Wendel said and took off his cap and held it with both hands. A tribute to an artist friend of mine. He passed.

He said his name, but I didn't recognize it.

Constructivist, said Wendel. He was a constructivist, Russian, actually Lithuanian, but he came to live here. He had a lot of ideas. A very original man.

Did he make this? I asked.

No, I put it together, Wendel said. It is a tribute.

Then he indicated another path with his arm and said: it's this way.

Wendel had bought the land almost twenty years ago. Since then he'd lived there all the time, summer and winter.

A stroke of luck, he said as he continued walking. I came one day by chance, I was going to visit some friends, I took the wrong highway and got lost. At that time there was another café-bar in town, one that later closed, and I stopped in to ask. I don't know how the subject of land parcels came up, and I had never thought about it before, but I asked them if there was anything around here for sale.

The quarry, they told me. The quarry is for sale.

That day I didn't even go to see it, but I left them my phone number.

A week later the owners called me. They said how they'd got my number, how they'd heard I might want to buy this piece of land.

I didn't know what to tell them, but I asked how much it cost, how many hectares it was. Five hectares, and at a price that was so low it sounded like a joke, I knew that much even though I didn't know anything else. With that money in Buenos Aires you couldn't get so much as a garage. I didn't even think about what I was doing, I just set up an appointment to go see him the next day.

I happened to have a little money, a small inheritance from my mother, Wendel said, and so I bought it. My daughters were horrified when they found out. What would I want something like that for? they said. How should I know what I wanted it for, said Wendel with a shrug. To be here, to come here, for this, Wendel said and pointed to all the trees around him, the forest, the grey trunks very still, the sun above.

I was old already, I was separated, one of my daughters was already married, the other was studying abroad. What was left for me there?

This land was scorched earth, not a blade of grass anywhere on it. That was the brickmakers, Wendel said. The kilns used to be here, from here they took the earth to make their bricks. It was the quarry. Until they used it all up. The plot was good, but very low, with all kinds of deep pits in it, they had sucked it dry. When I bought it, all there was was holes and trenches. In the end, if you add up all the truckloads of fill we had to put in to get it level, it cost me almost double: two garages, but even so, I don't have any regrets.

At that moment the path we were on took a turn and we came to another clearing, a clearing much larger than the other ones had been. I had to squint. The pale light of day blinded me. In the middle of the clearing, a garden, beds without weeds, neat rows, giant cabbages, a scarecrow in old clothes with a broom head, and in the centre, immense, spectacular, a large glass greenhouse, lit up by the sun, tall as a two-story house, with a gable roof.

And this? I asked.

This is my place, said Wendel.

Inside the air was hot and dense with humidity, with fetid vapour, fat drops of sweat dripping down the insides of the glass walls. Three lemon trees in giant pots grew in the centre, the heavy branches of lemons that were clenched like a fist, of an intense, almost phosphorescent yellow. Next to them, in other pots, palm trees, ferns that looked prehistoric, a cactus that rose almost to the top of the ceiling. The rest of the space was covered by benches and tables, all old, all different. And on them, very organized, always in a row and covering the entire surface, small flowerpots, yogurt containers, ice cream containers, containers from cream cheese, flan and desserts, oil drums cut in half, open Tetrabrik containers, milk bottles, wine bottles, all full of earth. In each one, the sprout of a plant. With a quick glance I came to recognize cypresses, oaks, pines, maples, ash trees.

Cypress seedlings! I said, unable to hide my surprise and enthusiasm.

Four or five different types, Wendel pointed out to me with a smile. White cypress or cypress-pine, he said, showing me one table. There's macrocarpa here, he said, showing me another. And here you have the funebris or the weeping cypress, as it's also called.

And over there are some casuarinas. I've got six varieties of oaks. And some ginkgos, there at that table, over by the entrance.

You grow trees, I said. Wendel nodded.

To sell?

No, I don't sell them.

What do you do with them? Why do you have so many?

Wendel shrugged.

Someday the brickmakers will use up the new quarry, too, he said and ran his fingers over the still fresh cotyledons of a newly germinated ash or maple.

I nodded.

They're seeds, Wendel said then and shrugged his shoulders again. Someone has to make them grow.

Telling stories to fill the void left by a home.
Or filling it with trees.

Little by little I go back to sowing, especially lettuce – oakleaf, butter, Batavia – red and green mizuna that Wendel gave me, more arugula, a little chicory. I plant a lot, very densely. If it doesn't freeze again, they might survive.

August 15, and it feels like the deep freezes may have passed. It still rains at least once a week, but it gets dark a little later every day.

An ancient ritual that celebrates the days getting longer. Celebrations that take place over twelve sunsets, to give thanks for that new daily minute of light.

The little acacia next to the vegetable garden has bloomed, and the one behind Luiso's shed is starting. A blaze of bright yellow flowers. Duckling yellow, lemon yellow, apple yellow, and the cadmium yellow that was such a favourite of Van Gogh's.

One of the Chinese cabbages has bolted, its flowers have a pale yellow inflorescence, similar to that of the tansy mustard but much larger. At siesta it fills up with bees.

Cold wind. Cloudy. I transplant more leeks, the Welsh onion, and I harvest some onions – the first – from the batch that survived the neighbour's pigs rooting around in their furrow. For lunch, I have pasta with garlic and sautéed kale. The garden is lovely, beds all clean after the stagnation and the weeds of winter. Arugula flowers, white, dancing single file in the wind. The calendulas are beginning to bloom, nice and orange. No delphiniums yet. I don't know if they're going to do anything or not. The cilantro comes up out of nowhere, the parsley I'd already given up on has stretched out and filled up with bright green leaves.

I make up some little pots and plant tomatoes, four different varieties, plus the Chinese ones from last year that I salvaged some seeds from. I plant eggplants, bell peppers and ñora peppers, some chili seeds I bought in Mexico a few years ago when I was invited to a book fair. I place the pots on the windowsill in the kitchen so they could be warmed by the afternoon sun. Planning, fantasizing about my summer garden.

Sunset is incredibly calm and quiet. Long. Such still air. It's like being inside an invisible fish tank, shut off from the void. I can make out only a few sounds, in the distance. Leeks growing in the dry poplar leaves. The arugula and the mustard have sprouted quickly. The curtain of poplars has not yet got green, it's still just grey stripped sticks. Its long, very long shadows over the field as the sun goes down more and more orange.

On my way to close the gate. It's cold. There's no moon, just a few stars. The lights of Lobos to the north, reflected off the low clouds. Those of Cañuelas to the south. A frog croaks, or is it crickets? The only audible thing is the sound of my footsteps in the grass. I walk at a good pace, regular, fast. The light of the flashlight illuminating the ground. When I return, a lapwing starts shrieking in the middle of the sheep's little pasture. Then he stops.

Why do we fall in love with the people we fall in love with? What could it be, what would we call those hidden buttons, those realms that are secret and inaccessible even to us, the receptors that light up when we're drawn to someone?

Does that realm in the darkest part of our body exist? Does that unknown button panel? What could its name be? What could it be like? Why do only certain smells, certain intonations, certain ways of looking, of moving, only certain sensibilities and not others press our buttons, and why are they and only they capable of making music sound?

What distant, prehistoric frictions do these new bodies remind us of? What do they echo?

And why do some people attract us to the point of insanity while others, who on paper meet all the conditions (they're cute in the way we find certain people cute, and they're deep, and funny, and pleasant to be around), manage to awaken in us only the very slightest tingle?

And how hard it is to say goodbye to them, how hard do we try, insist, give them one more chance after one more chance, because our mind tell us that this is the right person, but no: our days become a heavy taxiing for a vessel that cannot take flight.

Could I have been like that for Ciro? Seven long years of failing to push the right buttons? Can a misunderstanding last that long?

It still hurts, but in a calmer way. There are still certain things I can't go back to. Just as it's impossible for me to open the notebook I wrote when Ciro decided we needed to separate, I can't even think about going through my journals from the years we spent together, about rereading them, looking at them closely.

Even memories that come up suddenly, like flashes, knock me down if they catch me off guard. A certain gesture that appears to me in dreams. Certain smiles, a couple of the stories he would tell, certain objects, some parts or regions of his body that I remember suddenly, as though they were in front of me, present, palpable.

One day around noon, when we were already living in the new house. I had written all morning and had a couple of hours free before starting my afternoon workshops.

I went to the usual places: I had a coffee at my favourite café, I went to the grocery store and bought arugula, avocados, tomatoes, the first artichokes of the season. I went to the butcher's, and with a loaf of fresh bread in the bag that hung from my shoulder, I started for home, fully stocked, bags in both hands, lunch figured out. It was a very sunny day, but it wasn't hot. I remember perfectly which sidewalk I was on, which house I was in front of.

It was an instant. Suddenly, apropos of nothing, I was able to see myself from the outside and I understood that I was happy, completely happy. That happiness was those days, those routines, those squabbles over dirty clothes or who was supposed to water the plants, that 'I'll cook, you wash the dishes', that falling asleep as Ciro read, that joyful planning of what movie we were going to see in the theatre and what we were going to download from a torrent site to watch on Friday, stoned, after having fucked for a long time.

The tips of the grape ivy in the shed are beginning to swell. Purple, reddish buds. In a few days, not more than that, it will have leaves again.

The men have already resumed their work in the brick kilns. Today when I passed by there was a tractor in the yard, going around, mixing the mud. I haven't seen cutters yet, but the retro excavators were already making pits in the back, removing soil, digging.

Upon reaching the town, just before the square, I saw some of the willows were green again. The buds of the silver poplars by the chapel have sprouted tiny pompoms at their centres, white pompoms, soft as silk cocoons, velvety.

The kales have gone to seed. Something sad about that, a phase that is coming to an end.

Gorgeous day. Cool. Windows open. A sky so blue it dazzles. Everything calm. Silent. The doves coo. Every now and then, a bumblebee. Stillness. The cool veranda. The sun that beats down on the countryside but does not burn, only slightly warms.

Suddenly, a gust of wind.

I put cane stakes in with the delphiniums. The seeds weren't very good, few sprouted and only four or five survived. I cut down almost all the chard, since several of the plants look like they're about to bolt. With a little luck, they'll now grow a new batch of leaves before they're finished for good.

Orange butterflies with black splashes. Many, in the garden, with the bees hovering around the flowering kale.

The broccoli harvest is a complete failure. They take up a lot of space, and they only produced two or three minimal clusters. One of them never even formed a head. I pull them up and don't save the seeds because it isn't worth it. I'll have to get a different variety next year. I'll ask Wendel if he knows of any good ones.

The broad beans were another fiasco. They got overrun by aphids (twice). There they vegetate, without really going anywhere, and some of the stems start getting black and dry. I pull them before they've managed to produce any beans. Could I have planted them too early? Or were they affected by all that water?

Of the red cabbages there are three or four that refuse to come together. The Red Express variety has worked the best. Three nice hard heads have already formed. Another got the same plague of aphids that one of the first had had. I cut it and threw it into the trough, to burn it.

Of the oxheart cabbages, one is ready to be harvested. The other six aren't quite there.

The bare branches of the wisteria bloom. Flowers in heavy, long clusters, like crests that have fallen between the branches. An incredible colour, half light blue and half violet. While I read with the door open, at times the aroma of these flowers sneaks into the house and reaches the armchair, barely diluted. It's like a vapour. I move my head, trying to recapture it with my nose, but I can't find it anymore. It vanishes at once.

Luiso comes over with an update.

He sold the pigs, he says.

He's going around saying it's because he got tired of it, but the truth is that he didn't even have the feed for them. Nobody would give him credit.

What will he do now?

Luiso shrugs.

Who knows, he says.

What about your sister?

She started working as a janitor, at a school, my sister, says Luiso. She's happy.

When I walk against the wind, the wind roars in my ears and can be deafening. It blows my hair everywhere, it offers resistance, to make any progress I have to lean forward. On the other hand, if I turn and walk downwind, everything is fast and silent.

I like to walk against it, in order to feel like I'm making my way.

But I also like to walk downwind to feel that silence, the slight push of the wind on my back like a prize, a reward after my efforts.

The parrots have started building their nests in the highest part of the eucalyptus trees. They come and go all day, screeching and carrying twigs.

What about you, what are you doing here? Wendel asked me the other day, when I went to take him some Chinese tomato seeds.

I shrugged, didn't say anything.

How old are you?

Forty-two.

Wendel raised his head, looked at me.

You're too young to stay out here, he said.

I looked down.

I don't know, I said.

I do know, said Wendel and began to do something with the hoe, trace a better furrow, pull out a weed.

I'm not ready to leave yet, I said.

Wendel nodded.

It would still be best for you to go, he said.

I couldn't find trucks to bring my things last year,

before coming here, when I had just rented the house and started organizing the move. I had to vacate my friends' apartment as soon as possible, because the couple with two children who had rented it wanted to move in right away. I called all the moving companies I found and explained to them that the last stretch was twenty kilometres of dirt road: in that precise instant, all but one of them backed out. The one who gave me a quote wanted to charge me a fortune.

I told Luiso what was happening one day when I came to clean and plant the first things in the garden, and he told me about the quarry trucks. He handed me the manager's phone number.

He might be interested in a gig like that, he said.

I called him, and we came to an immediate agreement. The price was good, I could afford it. The only condition was that the move had to be done on a Sunday, because that was the day he didn't work.

I told Ciro and asked him to please pack up all my things, put my books in boxes, wrap in newspaper all the things I'd been collecting and growing over the years.

Until it was parked in front of what had been our house, I didn't understand that the truck they had offered me was a dump truck. The back part – the place where my things were going to travel – was just a metal box, the kind that tilts back thanks to a hydraulic ram, so that the soil pours out. It didn't even have a gate. There were no tarps to cover my books or bookshelves, and there was nowhere to attach any ropes to tie down my chairs, to keep them from flying away. Before starting to load the chairs, I swept the metal floor of the box with a broom and let the remains of grit and coarseness from its last trip fall onto the street.

The truck was very tall, the base of the box was almost at eye level, so lifting the packages required a lot of arm strength. Ciro helped me without saying a word. I saw his face when he realized what type of truck it was, but he didn't say anything.

The worst thing was trying to load the refrigerator without it flipping over, standing it upright, so that the cooling gas wouldn't escape.

Before leaving I asked the driver to be careful, not to accidentally touch the lever that raised the dump box or all my pots and plates and notebooks and furniture and books would end up everywhere, in the middle of the highway.

I said it as a joke, but he looked at me very seriously and said yes, that he would be careful, that there was no question of carelessness when it came to him.

I followed the truck in my car, twenty metres behind, the whole way. We went sixty on the highway. The journey seemed eternal. Toward the end of the afternoon, when we got onto the main road that goes to Zapiola, I saw a cloud of dust being kicked up by the wheels and rising behind the back of the truck, saw my things getting covered in dirt: dust forever settled into my books, my bookshelves, dust on my plates and cutlery, dust filling the cushions of my armchairs, the seats of my chairs, the top of my desk, my clothes, my pillows.

When we arrived, three of the brickmakers were waiting for us, and they helped us unload my boxes and leave them wherever, in the centre of the empty rooms, on the tiled floor, in that house in the middle of the field.

That first night I spent washing glasses, cups, pots, pans. With a damp cloth, I wiped down the pantry shelves and decided on places for everything: a shelf for food, a corner for spices. The first drawer is always for cutlery, dish towels in the second, while the third is the place for any junk that accumulates and that you don't know what to do with.

Starting a life somewhere else.

There was nothing, at first. When the first Juan arrived on the pampas.

There were no trees, there was nothing.

There was no shade, there was no protection, there was no shelter.

The air and the wind came from afar, gained momentum crossing that distance, hit hard, charged.

The first Juan had to make a fire with thistle sticks, straw, or dry cow dung.

Those were fragile fires, fires that couldn't be left alone for a second for fear they might go out.

They weren't even fire enough to heat a kettle.

There was land and there was water, but there were no bricks to make houses with. There wasn't any wood to use to fire them.

The first Juan built a mud shack. He cut the adobe rectangular and wide and left it to dry in the sun for weeks, praying that not a drop of water would fall from the sky.

A shack four leagues from the nearest town. A shack in the middle of nowhere. Two dogs. Three horses.

Some folks from Perdices let him go there to cut stakes: long willow branches, about a metre long, that he sank four or five buds on the stem of into the ground so that they would form roots.

He placed them in a straight line, spaced twelve metres apart, so that as they grew and thickened, they could also serve as fence posts.

Every day, the first Juan would walk down that line, eight hundred, nine hundred metres carrying buckets to water the stakes. He would kneel next to them, examine their buds, test them with his finger, try and see if they were going to sprout.

He protected them from the ants, the locusts, the worms. At night he went out to hunt snails with a lantern and a bucket.

He protected them, in winter, from the frost. He covered them up with rags. When they got bigger, he wrapped sections of burlap around their trunks.

And meanwhile, there he was, looking out at the countryside.

It wasn't worth sending any letter to Italy: they wouldn't believe him anyway.

There was also no one for him to send a letter to.

The very slow time in which a tree grows. Life passes by as he is waiting.

Until one day, finally, he could get his axe into it, chop it down, light up the oven, make the bricks, build a house.

It's the week of the bridal-wreath spiraea. All of them in flower. The rest of the year they're just nondescript bushes over there by the chicken coop and then, suddenly, one day, they transform. Big white balls, their branches hunched under the weight, forming arches, a shower of tiny petals washing over the grass.

The wisteria is done already. Its leaves have sprouted now. It has just a few flowers left, but they are lost among the green.

With the heat, the autumn carrots have started to bolt. There are still a few left to eat. The ones I planted last month are slow. They came up a little thin, but okay. I should have planted them earlier. Between the old ones being finished and the new ones starting to produce, it might be a while. A month or a month and a half of no carrots in the garden. At lunch, my first salad with the new lettuces. Mustard and mizuna and Galician lettuce. All from my thinning. The red swollen buds of the grape ivy have transformed into shiny leaves, with reddish tints and an apple-green base.

The back path covered with what looks like manzanilla horseweed. Lots of white flowers, with yellow centres. A stage effect, like in a movie. Water remains in the fields. Less of it than before, but it's still there. You can also see it running in ditches. Faster where there's a downward slope. Slowly the puddles shrink, and you begin to see the grass below, clinging to the ground but floating in the murky water, like the skeletons of jellyfish forming veils swayed by the current. Little by little, the water drains. The mosquitoes begin to trickle in.

The big hits of the autumn–winter season were the kale, the carrots, and the leeks.

The peas, the cauliflower, and the broad beans failed. The broccoli's paltry. The delphiniums barely came up. For next year I want to get some poppy seeds. I'll have to ask Wendel.

Where the broccoli and the cauliflower was, I sow the first batch of dwarf beans of the season. Last summer they yielded a lot, and now I love them: they aren't demanding, they don't take up much space, and they produce a good amount.

For the beans that need supports, I plan to wait a little longer for the cold to pass.

Meanwhile, where the broad beans were, I've planted zinnias, garden cosmos, more pincushion flowers, more chard, and beets again.

The garden full of bees and calendulas. I make a little bouquet and put it in a vase. I clean the desk, declutter it, put the old notebooks and notes in a box. Set down the vase in the middle.

First days of shorts and short sleeves. The new leaves of the poplars, a moist and fleshy green, shiny, delicate. If I squeeze them, they scar. When I was a child I used to leave messages on leaves, 'writing' them with the free edges of my fingernails. Every time I pressed, a part of a letter. One pinch for the upright stem of the E, three for the sideways arms. FEDE.

SEPTEMBER

Endings are the hardest part, says Hebe Uhart. It's always hard to say goodbye to someone you really loved.

The love of form is a love of endings, says Louise Glück.

That last talk with Ciro, that day at the café, when I was already living in the borrowed apartment, had already decided to move out to the country.

Everything that Ciro said.

He said: something had to give, we were stagnating, something had to explode.

He said: we've been living in a fortress, thinking we had no outside needs.

He said: at some point, I don't know how, that refuge became a kind of cage.

He said: we grew together, we made mistakes together, we fell into all the traps together, we saw each other at our darkest. It's hard to accept that someone knows us that well.

He said: sometimes people need a change, and they can't keep around witnesses to what came before.

He said: it was overwhelming me, it was making me anxious, it was scaring me, I always wanted to run away, and I was fighting that, until I couldn't.

He said: you were keeping our relationship going to such an extent that I couldn't figure out how to do it. Then I saw that you were down, close to a precipice. I knew that was my chance, and I didn't think twice: I pushed you.

He said: I can't be your family, you already have a family.

He said: what difference does it make how, what difference does it make how I did it, it was what I could do.

He said: how I did it was clumsy and awful, but the how is the least important thing of everything.

He said: our togetherness was so extensive there was nothing else it could do besides burst.

He said: it's okay that things fall apart sometimes because that's when something new shows up, that's when you make room for something new.

He said: we needed to separate so we could be ourselves.

He said: I know you're going to be okay.

He said: I apologize, forgive me.

He said: I'll never meet somebody like you again, someone who will make me feel the things you made me feel.

He said: our relationship was so vast that we'll always be linked.

He said: now each of us is going to move on with our lives and someday, many years from now, we're going to run into each other somewhere, at some birthday party, at some book launch, somewhere where there are lots of people, and we're going to look at each other across the crowd, and we're going to acknowledge each other with just the smallest gesture, and we won't even need to talk.

He said: I'm going to know all there is to know about you. You're going to know all there is to know about me. You're always going to be the only person in the world who really knows me.

I said: there were the two of us/it was the both of us.

I said: you're not my partner any longer, you won't be part of me anymore.

Unfurling the leaves, the wind murmurs down the row of trees again, sounding, at every gust, the poplars.

They sway in the wind. These trees are elastic.

The bridal-wreath spiraea keeps blooming and blooming, but there are more and more fallen petals around it now. They last just a little while. Almost immediately they curl in on themselves and turn yellow, as if oxidized, like apples.

It's getting dark. I go to close the gate. On hearing my footsteps, the two hares jump and shoot across the field.

First, few, fireflies out here.

I harvest the last red cabbage in the garden. Small head, but tightly packed. I cut it into very thin strips and let them soak. The water gets dyed a deep blue, almost indigo. The same blue-grey tint as the leaves over the winter. I eat it in a salad.

Luiso and I worked in the garden all day, with no breaks. We made two new beds for tomatoes and two more for the peppers and the eggplants. We decided to split the land, become partners in the summer garden. He says I have a green thumb, and that the soil at his place isn't as good as it is here. And it's good for me, too, since this way if I have to leave, go out of town for a few days, spend a few days a week in Buenos Aires, Luiso will water for me.

We loosened the soil and dug, and at some point, Luiso stopped to rest.

What are we going to do with so many tomatoes? he said and wiped his forehead with his forearm.

Sixty tomato seedlings. Twenty eggplants. Fourteen chili peppers. Ten more of the chilis and neither one of us likes spicy food.

It's just me and my wife in my house, Luiso said. My little girl doesn't like tomatoes, she won't eat them.

I shrugged.

I don't know, Luiso. I don't know, I told him. We'll figure it out later on.

Making a drawing: tying together all the thistles in a field, one by one, with a very long red string, so that it stands out against the green of them.

Whatever thistles there are. In any order. Tie the thistles. Whichever ones you want, or can, or manage to spot, and it will turn out however it turns out.

In the late afternoon, I take out the lounge chair and start reading under the eucalyptus trees. I let out the hen so she can walk around as she pleases for a while. I don't pay attention to her and focus on the book.

A silence filled with birds. The parrots that continue to build their nests in the eucalyptus trees. Pigeons that coo. Other little birds. A chimango that flies overhead and ends up landing on one of the corners of my house.

The common jasmines covered in buds about to bloom. Smell of jasmine, of lavender, the very sweet smell of the flowers on the chinaberry tree.

In the background, around, always nearby, I hear the hen as she digs, clucks quietly, as though talking to herself, searching for something in the grass with her feet.

Suddenly, she lets out a high-pitched note, almost a squawk. She clucks loudly, as though surprised or frightened.

I turn to see what's going on.

She has laid her first egg, right there, warm, on the grass.

Tying yourself to something.

To a vegetable garden, a forest, a plant, a word.

Tying yourself to something that has a root, tying a knot so as not to get lost in the wind that blows over the pampas and calls.

Some people, when their lives fall apart, go back to their parents' houses. Others don't have anywhere to go back to.

I went back to the country.

I built a garden to fill the void.

The gaping void of time.

Time without narrative, without stories. Plains time.

I sit down at my desk. I move the little bouquet of orange calendulas to one side.

I open my notebook. I look at my handwriting. Everything I have written these past few months, this time in the country.

Putting one word after another simply as a way to be.

Telling yourself a story to try and be at peace.